## P.C. Tony Ragl
## LB 265

"What the bloody hell are you playing at, mate?"

I pulled out of the turnaround that fronted Poets' End pier – Lothing had two piers, one either end of the stretch of beach, but only the southern most one had been graced with an elegant name, and a bit of investment. The other, despite sitting alongside the marina, was simply referred to by its beach and location - "North Beach" - and was languidly languishing towards dilapidation.

Lothing was a town of contrasts, but I wasn't interested in that, right now. Right now, the only thing I was interested in was the blue Ford Escort that had shot past the Area Car like a bat out of Hell. It was three a.m on a weekday, otherwise the lunatic behind the wheel wouldn't have had a hope of getting up that kind of speed – on this stretch of road, or any other in Lothing.

Feroc hit the lights and sirens without even a glance from me. "Lima Bravo from Lima Bravo One, show us in pursuit of a blue Ford Escort, registration number Foxtrot Victor Zero Two, Uniform Romeo Delta, heading North, at speed, along London Road. Over."

"Received, Lima Bravo One. Shown in pursuit, target vehicle blue Ford Escort, Foxtrot Victor Zero Two, Uniform Romeo Delta. All units, copy those details: repeat, copy attention requested blue Ford Escort, registration Foxtrot Victor Zero Two, Uniform Romeo Delta, vicinity London Road, heading North. Lima Bravo One in pursuit, all other units, do not interrupt pursuit, repeat, all other units, stay clear of Lima Bravo One. Over."

I smiled. We'd got engaged a few weeks before my forty-sixth birthday, and our commitment ceremony was planned for six months hence, the thirteenth of October, a year and a day from our engagement. The timing was deliberate, though more Wiccan than Heathen. Heathenry would have wondered why we needed to plan a pledging of an oath of fidelity, and, if it accepted that we *did* need to plan it, would wonder why it was taking so long.

"What the -" I flicked my gaze down at the speedometer, then up at the dashcam, making sure the latter was recording the details that had led to what I seen on the former. "They're doing over a ton! They must be – Shit! No!"

Feroc had clearly heard the short, sharp yelp of the sirens at the same moment I did. Beside me, he paled, and shook his head slowly as he keyed the mic.

"Lima Bravo from Lima Bravo Five-Nine-Nine, suspect vehicle is heading towards the Bascule Bridge, still at speed. The sirens have just gone off. Repeat, suspect vehicle clocked at over one-hundred, that's one, zero-zero, mph, and the warning sirens for the raising of the Bascule Bridge have just sounded. Over."

"Received Five-Nine-Nine. Over." Aimee Gardiner's voice was flat, without any of her usual cheerful breeziness. This, most definitely, was business.

"Lima Bravo One from Lima Bravo, I'm dispatching India Nine-Nine to your location, over."

"Copy – bloody *hell!*"

The car wasn't even beginning to slow down for the rising bridge. Ahead – too damn close – I could see the white silhouettes of the barriers falling into place. And still the Escort wasn't slowing down.

With a primal yell that was pure adrenaline, I flung Lima Bravo One onto the pavement, sending a couple of night-shift Port Authority workers diving backwards against the safety of the metal fencing, and, rubber burning, wheels screeching, engine whining in protest, arced her round, swinging wide in front of the Escort.

The driver didn't have time to stop. The Escort ploughed into the back of the Area Car, slamming us forward with a force that felt like a bomb blast. I heard the tearing of metal and the shattering of glass as the barrier broke, one end of the top rail smashing through the window. I jerked my head back, eyes rolling, like I was a horse about to bolt.

The Escort's velocity had sent its nose clear through the back door, shoving Feroc's seat forward. There was a hair's breadth between his pelvis and the dashboard. I closed my eyes, not wanting to picture what so easily could have been. When I opened them again, I saw the face of the Escort's driver, inches from my shoulder, eyes wide with shock.

It was the pale, lined face of an elderly woman, the blood that trickled from her temple seeming too stark, too bright, against the permed, pale grey of her wiry hair.

In a daze, I keyed the mic. "Lima Bravo from Lima Bravo One, we've had a POL-AC, over. Oh, and the bridge took a bit of a hit. Someone should probably sort that out." I started laughing, the shrill, staccato laugh of the deranged. Feroc tried to call my name – at least I think he was trying to call my name. He just ended up opening and closing his mouth, no sound, just breath, and shaking his head over and over and over again.

The driver of the Escort started sobbing.

I could feel the unique pain that immediately announced itself as whiplash, and, without surprise, as though I were looking at a sepia photograph, I noticed that my seatbelt had sheared clean through. That took almost unprecedented force. The airbags had inflated, although, at that speed, they hadn't done much good. My chest felt like it was on fire, and I knew, in a couple of days, I'd have a map of multi-coloured bruises.

I let my eyes wander, hoping that taking a visual stroll through the scene would somehow make it less real, or at least show me a simple, obvious way I could get us all out of this, put the bridge barrier back into one piece, and get everyone home, preferably with a body in the back of the Area Car, even if it was just an old dear done for speeding. You never know, maybe she was fleeing the scene of a mass murder, having finally lost her temper with whatever passed for elderly care these days. In the corner of my vision, darker black against the blue-black, greying dawn, the hull of the *Sea Alpha*, a research vessel that was registered and domiciled in Lothing, hove into view. I could see the shadowy shapes of crew members on deck, and the ship was travelling far slower than she should have been: clearly, *Sea Alpha* had heard the crash on the bridge, or seen something on her approach.

I wondered if *Sea Alpha* intended to stop and render assistance: she was too large to moor in the inlet beneath the bridge, and, the seaward side, the only mooring large enough to take her in the marina was the historic vessels mooring, which was already occupied by *Mincarlo*. *Sea Alpha* would either have to take the long route round, through Lake Lothing, and back to her own home berth, or moor in tidal waters, which she was more than equipped to do.

A uniform was approaching, too hesitantly to be a copper. Coppers are the fools who rush in where angels fear to tread. This guy was walking with sensible wariness, looking as if he might, at any moment, change his mind and make a run for it.

*Thank the Gods,* I heard my brain mutter. *Someone else to deal with this crap.*

The radio yelped into life, causing me to slur a profanity, as though I were some Saturday night drunk, angry at being disturbed by the forces of law and order.

"Lima-Bravo One from Lima-Bravo Eight One, what the hell's happening out there? Lima-Bravo One? Tony? Two-Six-Five from Eight-One, what's happening, over? Five-Nine-Nine? This is Inspector Wyckham – sit rep, please. Tony? Feroc? One of you answer me, dammit!"

*Later,* I thought, then drowsily added *Sorry, Guv.*

I glanced at Feroc, and saw a bead of red crawling slowly down his white face.

Then everything went black.

5

## Captain Martin Briggs
### *Sea Alpha*

"Captain – you need to see this! There's been a bad smash, up on the bridge!"

I turned to my second in command. "Lewis, take over here, would you?" He saluted, and moved smartly into the position I'd already vacated. I'd heard an almighty smash, and a lot of shouting, just as we were drawing level with the bridge. It hadn't sounded like a run of the mill accident then, and it didn't now, expressed in gabbling shock from the lips of a junior crewman.

I hurried after him. At three a.m, on a weekday morning, my crew and I may well be the only witnesses to whatever had happened that weren't caught up in it. I didn't want to acknowledge the thought that followed that – that we may be the only witnesses *alive.*

"What happened? Car overshot and hit the barrier? He'll have been speeding, if that's the case."

"I think it's worse than that, Captain – I saw blue lights on the bridge."

My mind instantly flashed back eighteen months, to the bar area of the Heart of Darkness. I'd been enjoying a quick drink before heading home, having just got back to port that day, when... Well, everyone in Lothing knew what had happened that day. The front page photo had been Tony Raglan, curled up in a foetal position, bleeding out on the wood effect laminate after some maniac had gutshot him. They'd taken the guy down – some lowlife drug dealer, apparently – and he was safely inside. But it was an old superstition that misfortune weakened you. That, once something bad happened to you, bad things kept happening to you, misfortune being drawn by the original injury.

All I hoped, as we ran, was that there hadn't been a car go *off* the bridge. We'd never get out even close to schedule if that were the case. And, of course, it meant someone would certainly be dead, and friends and family would be woken to shock and grief.

I followed Malcom Laven to a point towards the stern, and peered up into the gloom.

I saw the blue light and white livery of the police car, but there was something wrong about it, something I couldn't make out. Something about the shape of it.

Someone ran up with an arc lamp, and I realised what was wrong: there was a second car, clean through the back of the police car. I couldn't see who was driving either car, but I knew instinctively Tony Raglan was the copper behind the wheel, and I hoped like hell he got out of this in one piece. He was a good copper, a good man. Lothing, whether it realised it or not, needed him.

It had been a shock when people started saying Raglan was gay, that he'd taken up with some young copper – the blond haired kid who'd been there at the Heart of Darkness that night. Neither of them seemed like the kind of people you imagined batting for the other side, but I suppose it takes all sorts. And being gay certainly didn't mean you deserved this kind of bad luck.

Because, whatever had gone before, that's what this looked like: nobody's fault, just sheer bloody bad luck.

## Inspector Bill Wyckham
## LB 81

I threw the headset down, and turned to Aimee Gardiner. "What's Lima-Bravo One's last known location?"

"Sir -" David Hearn, a young Constable, interrupted "- we've just had a call from Jack Alfram, the Harbour Master. Apparently there's been an accident on the Bascule Bridge." He paused. "He said he thinks there's a police car involved."

Aimee Gardiner looked up. "Sir – we've just had a call from a Port Authority worker, Kenny Tracer. Lima-Bravo One's been hit. Full on. There's an Escort clean through the back of them." She gave a weak, shaky smile. "But, on the upside, Tony Raglan was able to call it in."

"And now he's not answering his radio – either his PR, or the main set."

"Sir." I turned to David. His face looked green. I'd always thought that was a myth, that people went green from shock, but, looking at David Hearn, it clearly wasn't.

"David?"

"Sir, Jack Alfram – they're right up against the bridge."

I felt my blood drop several degrees. "You don't mean -"

He nodded.

"God." It came out as a moan, not a prayer. I closed my eyes.

As a copper, you spend a lot of time dealing with the dead, but they're usually strangers, unless something goes badly wrong on the beat. The last person I'd known, personally, who'd died had been my Mum, twelve years ago. Cancer.

People talk of "fighting" cancer, but my mother hadn't. She'd listened to the diagnosis, looked up at the consultant, and asked "Is there any hope at all? Anything you can do that won't make me feel worse?"

The consultant had been a mature woman, tired-looking yet kindly. She'd been upfront with Mum, shaking her head sadly. "I'm afraid it's too advanced for any sure-fire treatments. All we could do is try -"

"No." My mother's quiet voice had been firm. "Not chemotherapy. I won't go through that."

The consultant hadn't tried to talk her round. She had simply nodded, and shaken her hand.

"Good luck Marian."

My mother had smiled, and, as she'd stepped out into the corridor, had turned to us – me, my father, my brother – and said simply: "I've had a good life – a wonderful life. God has blessed me with so many friends, a loving husband, two beautiful boys. I've had hobbies I've enjoyed, and memories that have lasted me a lifetime. But that lifetime is at an end, now. And I understand that. I'm ready for it."

She'd taken my father's hand, and gazed up into his eyes. "I love you, John."

He'd bent down, kissed her on the lips, light as a butterfly. "I love you, too, Marian."

My brother and I had smiled at each other, remembering the number of times that people had joked "Who'd've thought that Maid Marian would end up married to Little John." I also remembered my father's response on one such occasion: "Isn't it obvious that it's always been Little John that Marian loved?"

John Wyckham had survived his wife by a decade, dying peacefully in his sleep the day before Tony Raglan was shot.

My father's last words to me, the morning of the day he died, had been eerily prescient: "Take care of that lad Raglan, Billy. He's hurt, somehow, and he needs someone who'll patch him up, dose him, and keep an eye to him."

I'd laughed. "Tony Raglan can take care of himself, Dad."

My Dad had taken my arm, holding on with both his hands. "Bill – appearances can be very deceptive. You should know that better than anyone. And Tony Raglan's become very, very good at keeping up appearances." He'd paused. "And you don't pick up those kind of skills casual-like. They're taught by hard, violent lessons. The kind that leave scars." Dad had let go of my arm, but not my gaze. "You'll need him, one day."

"The Force always needs experienced coppers."

"Not the Force, Billy – you."

"I can't see that being the case, Dad. Tony Raglan's a hellion – sent by the devil himself, I'd swear it, sometimes."

"Ah, but even the devil is a part of God, Billy."

As I ran through the corridors of the station, heading for the back yard, and my car, I thought about Tony and Feroc. I'd never had openly Heathen coppers on one of my teams, and I wasn't sure what gods, if any, they followed. But I sent out a prayer, or whatever the likely candidates for Heathen devotion would want, as I reached my car.

*Whomever, whatever, is called on by Tony and Feroc, be with them now. Bring them through this. Go to them. Save them, Shield them.*

As I got into my car, sweat clammy on my hands, my vision blurring with what couldn't have been tears, because I didn't cry, I couldn't help worrying that I might have been too late. That it might have been too late for quite a while.

As I pulled out of the yard, a raven – or a crow, I'd never been able to tell the difference – circled low overhead, then swept upwards to meet another of its kind. Together, they flew off, heading towards the bridge.

The scene was chaos, but the kind of chaos that tells you the professionals are there, that you don't need to worry, that everything is being taken care of. That it's going to be alright.

As I drove along Chambers Road, past the marina, I could see the deck lights of the CEFAS ship *Sea Alpha.* I assumed the hi-vis figures were *Sea Alpha's* crew, forming a temporary road block.

I couldn't see anything up ahead. The crash must have happened the other side of the bridge, on the London Road side. I pulled my car over, as a man in orange overalls came towards me.

"Inspector Wyckham."

I recognised the man, and smiled. "Martin."

Martin Briggs, Captain of the Sea Alpha, and I had been friends for several years. Our daughters attended the same school, and were both into horses – in the riding, not the betting, sense. We usually hacked out together, our two families, along the coast road at least once a month.

"Your lads the other side of the bridge?"

I nodded.

"Bad business."

"How are they?"

He shook his head. "I don't know, Bill. But I've got more of my crew blocking that end. Do you want to go round that way?"

"Yes."

"I hope it's alright, Bill."

"You and me both."

"Nothing's been moved – Jack Alfram said you'd..."

"Want to see everything in situ? Yes. That's the way."

I took a deep breath, and raised my radio. "Lima-Bravo from Eight-One, request mobile units and Traffic to the London Road side of the Bascule Bridge on Commercial Road. As well as ambulances and the brigade."

"Received."

I heard the near-distance whine of sirens, and I imagined I could see the ghosts of the mobile units I'd requested, running to the bridge.

I jogged back to my car, got in, turned around, and drove away, taking the long, anxiety-inducing route round to the other side of the bridge. It would only take five, ten minutes at most, but, as I drove, my mind picturing Tony and Feroc, not knowing what kind of state they were in, I knew it would feel like an eternity.

As I came round onto London Road, I saw the circling blue lights, and the white glare of India Nine-Nine's search light. That white glare highlighted the tall, lean figure of Jack Alfram, Harbour Master.

I pulled up a hundred yards back from the scene, and got out of the car as Alfram came over.

"Wyckham."

"Alfram."

We shook hands. I glanced towards the bridge. Alfram nodded.

"You want to see them."

"Are they -"

"It looks bad, but I think they're alright. Or they will be, once the medics have had some time with them. Not so sure about the old dear in the Escort, though."

"Old dear? That can't be right – their last transmission said they were in hot pursuit. At speed. A speeding car."

"Well, she's gone right through the back of them, ripped a hole where the back seats ought to be. She'd have to have been driving at some kind of whack to achieve that. From the position of the cars, I'd say your boys pulled round in front of her to try and stop her hitting the barriers as they came down. Your driver was very brave."

"Or very foolish."

Alfram studied me. "Was the driver Tony Raglan?"

I nodded.

"Bad luck."

"Yes. I can't help thinking -"

Alfram laid a hand on my arm. "Look, Wyckham, I doubt anyone's going to go after Tony Raglan with a gun because one old lady got confused about the brake and the accelerator."

"I never thought anyone would go after any of my team with a gun for what happened two years ago."

Alfram nodded. "I understand, Wyckham. But your boy knows how to handle himself."

"I need to see them."

"Of course."

I headed towards the scene at the same speed I approached restless crowds – more than a jog, less than a run, more purposeful than both. My heart was hurling itself against my chest, and I couldn't shake the image of Tony and Feroc, trapped in the Area Car.

The first thing I saw was the torn, jagged end of the top bar of the right hand barrier slammed clean through the driver's side window.

Someone, somewhere in the pre-dawn light, someone screamed a single name:

*"TONY!!!"*

I realised, with a cold shock, that the person screaming was me.

"Inspector Wyckham? Catherine Anderson. Senior Brigade Officer. Is that your boy in there?"

I gasped for breath, fighting to stop screaming. "Yes. Tony. Tony Raglan. And Feroc. Feroc – what's going to happen to Feroc if Tony dies?"

"He's not going to die, Inspector."

"Why haven't you got him out of the car yet?"

She took a deep breath. "We can't. Not until the bridge comes down. It's not safe. We're waiting for a structural engineer to come out, to assess whether it *can* be brought down. There doesn't appear to be any damage, but we can't take the risk."

"I want my boys out."

"I do understand, Inspector, but it can't happen yet."

"I want to see them."

She nodded, and stepped forward, arm outstretched, gesturing that I should follow her.

Instead, I pushed ahead, trying not to run. Trying not to scream out Tony's name, Feroc's name. A steady hand on the tiller. That's what they'd need. Through this, after this.

I turned back to Catherine. "What's it look like? Be honest with me."

She sighed. "Tricky."

My heart slowed. *Tricky* wasn't good. *Tricky* meant people could be seriously injured. People could be dead. *Tricky* meant a long, stressful night.

"If it helps, we should be able to get the police passenger out fairly quickly. Getting him free doesn't rely on the bridge coming down."

I took a breath. "That's good."

"You don't look like it is."

"The driver -"

"Ah. It's those officers, is it? The two who got together after the shooting?" Her face softened.

I nodded. "Yes. Feroc Hanson and Tony Raglan. Tony – he's been through too much already." I scanned her face, seeing something there I never wanted to see at a scene, any scene, least of all this one. "What's wrong? What's happened to Tony?"

"Nothing -"

 I was running now, the last few yards of ground falling away under my feet. "Inspector!"

I reached the car, crouching down beside the driver's side. I jerked my head up and back, wild eyes staring at Catherine Anderson. "He's unconscious!"

"Yes. It's nothing to worry about -"

"Nothing to worry about!"

"It's the brain's way of protecting itself, in traumatic situations. It's actually beneficial for the healing process."

I took a deep breath – and saw Feroc turn to face me.

"Guv."

"You'll be alright Feroc. You'll both be alright."

 In the gathering light, I heard a too-familiar voice. "What the bloody hell's the daft idiot done now?"

## Sergeant Harry Beresford
## Traffic

"Bloody hell." I stood in the lightening gloom, the rhythmic bass notes of the sea to my right keeping time with the pounding that was starting up in my head.

On pure reflex, without any conscious thought or effort of will, I took out my smartphone and began snapping what I called "spec pics", unedited, unfiltered first impressions, recorded for whatever kind of posterity an incident report can hope for. I'd get the professional gear out of the boot in a minute, start taking continuous video, but I liked my immediate shots. They often told you far more about a scene than the video, even though that shouldn't have been possible. Small cameras caught things larger lenses missed.

My first impressions of the scene? It could easily have been a hell of a lot more serious, and given how serious it was, that was saying something.

I walked over to the driver's door of the Area Car. Tony Raglan was slumped forward, his normally ruddy face pale. Blood was slowly sliding around the end of the battered pole that was rammed through his side. When I'd been looking at the scene from a distance, I'd thought the pole had just gone through the window. That's why video and photo evidence alone were no good. It was why you had to get up close and personal, right in the face of everything that was wrong with the scene. Because, from a distance, things sometimes looked alright, or at least not all that bad. From a distance, mistakes were made.

Tony had been unlucky – a millimetre lower, and the pole would have bounced off his stab vest. As it was, having gone in through the arm holes, it was unlikely to have snagged anything major.

But, of course, 'unlikely' didn't translate to 'definitely wouldn't have done.' He needed a medic, sooner rather than later. Which meant we needed that bloody structural engineer out here to give the all clear for the bridge to be brought down sooner rather than later.

I brushed away fragments of glass with an unhanded glove, and leaned in, touching my fingers to Raglan's forehead.

It felt cold and clammy. Not nearly human enough. Not nearly *alive* enough.

Feroc stirred, and turned his head, moaning in pain. He blinked, struggled, and finally managed to speak. "Beresford. What's going on? Sorry. Sarge. What's going on, Sarge?"

"They're waiting for a structural engineer. They need the all clear to lower the bridge. Then they'll have the space to work on the driver's side of the car."

"Tony -"

Before I could answer, a paramedic jogged up. "Excuse me." She knelt where I'd been standing moments ago, and leaned through the same shattered glass to do a vital-signs check. Something caused her to frown, and she wasn't quite quick enough to turn away.

Feroc caught the look.

"What is it?" His voice was an octave higher than I was used to, and his eyes had the wild gleam of the insane, the gleam of someone with several voices all shouting at once. "What's wrong? Tony!"

The paramedic glanced up, and tried for a reassuring smile that didn't quite come off. "Everything's fine. Your colleague's going to be okay. There's nothing to worry about."

The oxygen mask she slid over Tony's face, cutting herself as she leaned through the broken window, twisting to avoid bumping up against the broken pole of the barrier rail, and potentially causing more damage, gave the lie to that statement.

Quietly – so quietly I would have missed it if I hadn't been looking straight at him – Feroc Hanson began to cry.

## P.C. Feroc Hanson
## LB 599

I was surprised how quietly the tears came. Normally, when I cry
– which is maybe once every three years, or something like that –
it's a major performance: snot everywhere, choking sobs, red face,
the works. This, though, was the kind of crying that happened
when you peeled onions. Only without the onions.

Of course, Tony *would* pick that moment to regain
consciousness. That's the most awkward thing about being gay,
for me: letting your partner see you cry. A woman crying, either in
front of a man who loves her, or in front of her girlfriend, triggers
the urge to protect, in the case of the male, or to befriend and
shelter, in the case of another woman. Either way, she's wrapped
up in loving arms, her hair is smoothed away from her tear-filled
eyes, and someone rocks her, whispers sweet nothings to her.

As a man crying in front of other men, though, you always feel a
bit of a prat, a bit of a loser. Boys don't cry, we tell our sons, and
they carry that lesson with them, amplified by painful experiences
of the times they've broken that particular commandment, into the
world of men.

"Oh, good. You're back with us. You had us worried for a
moment."

I didn't recognise the woman's voice. A blur of green jumpsuit
told me it was the paramedic I'd seen before – she must have
spoken to me then, I remembered her seeming worried about
Tony, but her voice was completely unfamiliar to me.

"The car – oh, stars and stones. Wyckham's going to kill me. The
car's a mess."

"It's a write-off, I'm afraid. But you're alright, and so's your
colleague. That's all that matters now."

Tony gave a short laugh, and a yelp of surprised pain. "That's
what you think."

"Try and keep still. And put that mask back on, please."

I hadn't seen Tony reach up to pull the oxygen mask away, but I
wasn't surprised he had – he hated having anything over his face.

"You need to work on your pole routine though, Raglan – you're supposed to drape seductively around it, legs in the air. Not just get shanked through the side."

"Screw you, Beresford." Through the oxygen mask, Tony sounded like Darth Vader. Despite everything, despite my worry about Tony, despite the look of the old dear who'd shoved her car snout-first into the back of us, despite the half-light of coming morning, and the strange shapes it was creating, I laughed.

Then, I glanced across at Tony, and abruptly stopped. I could hear him breathing – too slow, too shallow. I would have sworn in Court, would have sworn on all my ancestors, that I could see the veins beneath the skin of the man I loved.

His eyelids fluttered – I wondered if there was more than oxygen being run through that mask. Despite my own agony, the blaze of white hot pain every time I moved, I reached out, and laid a hand on his shoulder. "You're going to be okay. We're going to be okay."

Tony glanced over his shoulder without moving his head, eyes rolling like a frightened horse's. I followed his gaze.

The old lady in the Escort, the reason for all of this, was slumped forward, her face tissue white. She was too still, too silent. If she was alive at all, it was barely.

Suddenly, there was a racket of movement, the slamming of a car door, raised voices slashing through the silent dawn.

"Bloody hell – you weren't joking when you said it was urgent, were you?"

"We don't make a habit of sending out wild shouts and dragging structural engineers out of their cosy beds at sparrow-fart for trivial matters, Mr. Truder."

"No, I'm sure you don't." Right, let's get a look at it, then – lads, couple of you over the other side, please. Alex, with me."

I wondered if Alex was a *der* or a *dra*. I never found out. I suddenly felt very tired, very cold, and, before I was fully aware it was happening, my eyes closed, and there was only darkness, and silence. And Tony.

It was all, always, about Tony: first, last, forever.

### Ralph Truder

The UK has twenty Bascule bridges, of which London's Tower Bridge is the most famous. It saddened me, whenever I read in the local press of the resentment of Lothing's residents towards their specimen – after all, there wouldn't be traffic congestion if more people got off their backsides and walked or cycled. Or took the plentiful buses that ran into and around the town, or the trains that ran out of it to Norwich, Ipswich, and London. Although they moaned about the railway crossings, too. Anything that reminded human beings that, despite all their "progress", all their technology, all their ease and luxury, they were not gods, was on the hit list for a good old moan, preferably in the Letters pages of the local rag.

 I got out of my car, and stretched. Norwich was an ache-inducing drive, even though it took less than an hour to get to Lothing from there. I ignored the crash site, walking directly past it without so much as a glance. My mind was already on the underside of the bridge, and in particular the hinge mechanism. It didn't look, from the position of the cars, as though anything vital would have been damaged, apart from the barriers – we'd need to have them removed from their housing before the bridge came down, and we'd certainly be annoying the residents by closing this stretch of road for however long it took for replacements to arrive – the people of Lothing hated the bridge, but they hated being denied its convenience even more.

 As I drew level with the underside of the bridge, where Alex was already setting up the small telescopic basket that would take us directly under the bridge, mounted on a pavement-based tripod, I stopped, and pulled on the orange hi-vis overalls I'd been carrying with me. Alex handed me a hard hat. The blue probably clashed with the orange, but nobody was here to take part in a fashion parade.

 Alex brought the basket as low as it would go, and, with the usual slight, ungainly effort, I clambered aboard.

 A flick of Alex's wrist, some controls tapped, and we were

swinging forward, the early-morning breeze rocking the basket as
it travelled into the looming shadow of the bridge.

I hoped the bridge was safe. If the slab of tarmac above us gave
way, there was no hope for us. The water below looked dark, cold,
and deeply threatening. The concrete banks loomed steeply into
the dawn skyline.

With torches, and in the harsher light of arc lamps, I studied the
hinge mechanism, and glimpsed my colleagues doing the same on
the other side. We were fortunate that it was only one half of the
bridge we needed to worry about.

Everything seemed in order, but there was only one way I would
know for certain. I nodded to Alex to bring the basket back to the
pavement, and, once the inevitable swaying had stopped, I stepped
out, and signalled to one of the uniforms present.

He jogged over, a look in his eyes that said the officers in the
police car were more than just numbers and salaries to him.

"Tell them they can start lowering the bridge. I'll need to watch it
come down before I can definitely give you the all-clear."

"But you think it's going to be alright?"

"I can't be a hundred percent until I've seen it come down."

The man frowned, then ran over to someone in a hi-vis suit
similar to my own, but with a better-matched hard hat – his was
white. The white hat bobbed once, twice, and the orange blur
moved purposefully away. Moments later, metal moaned, and
tarmac slabs of road began to fall from the sky.

I loved watching heavy, solid structures in flux, particularly
where metal was involved. I loved listening to the conversations
between hinges and joints, struts and braces, load, resistance, and
accommodation, as everything shuddered and groaned its way into
position. It was like watching a thoroughbred racehorse clear the
winning post on Grand National day, only without the
disappointment of dashed hopes for those who'd backed other
beasts.

We made this. Humans took raw materials that had no prior
connection to one another, materials that could have been
anything, and used our own ingenuity, creativity, and sheer plucky

determination, to bring them together and forge something new, something powerful, something noble. We took base material, and turned it into a kind of gold. A kind of god. That, to me, was the beauty and wonder of humanity: the fact that we had never stopped building Babel.

With a final resonant clang, like a shot echoing through eternity, a bellow of a structure's triumph over its constructors, the two halves of the bridge fell back into place, the road lying smooth and flat in the pale light of a day that was dawning, however dark things had seemed to the waiting humans.

On the other side, my team gave a thumbs up. The uniformed officer was back beside me, his expression hopeful.

"It all seems fine. Tell everyone they can be about their jobs." I turned to walk back to my car, then paused. "I hope your men are alright."

"So do I, " the officer replied, his eyes holding both fire and tears. "I bloody well hope everyone's alright – my boys, and the woman who caused this."

## Inspector Bill Wyckham
## LB 81

I wasn't used to feeling helpless, and it certainly wasn't a feeling I
wanted to *become* used to. Watching as other men and women,
from other emergency services, worked on in the gathering light, I
was uncomfortably aware that there was nothing I could do.

I'd always been proud of the fact that I was there for the officers
under my command, that, whether their problem was the Job, their
life outside it, or the fact that they felt they didn't *have* a life
outside it, I'd been the first to offer help, the first to come up with
solutions. Sometimes, the first to do something practical. I
realised now, watching a scene I had no part in, that Tony Raglan
had never made it possible for me to help him. He'd kept his own
counsel, always. If he'd had any problems, he'd either resolved
them himself, or ignored them. I hadn't even known he was gay,
for crying out loud, and he'd apparently had a troubled and
troubling lover before Feroc.

And this was the second time he'd been close to death, and yet
again, just like the first, I wasn't able to help him.

At a loss for anything else to do, I walked away, crossed the road
just beyond the other side of the bridge, and headed down to the
seawall.

On the pier head, men in hi-vis suits were emptying the public
bins, and, father out, what looked like a fishing boat was rounding
the curve the horizon created, heading for the docks. Just visible
along the horizon were two large, ghost-shaded vessels, sitting
quietly, watching, waiting. I felt a shiver of unease, even though I
knew they were probably simply conducting a fuel transfer, or
waiting for full light before continuing their journey. When had
we started to worry about shadowy figures keeping watch?

My gaze drifted back to the men working on the bins, and I
smiled as I remembered Tony Raglan, responding to a foolish
young copper who'd suggested women weren't strong enough to
be coppers, because "you never saw them doing hard graft."
Tony's voice, rich and deep, with a flint edge to it, rolled through

my awareness with the waves.

"No, you don't. But you do see them carrying ten bags of groceries, two kids, and pushing a third in a buggy, getting it all up four flights of council-flat stairs single-handed. It's not that women aren't strong enough: it's that they're not daft enough. We run around wanting to prove we're real men, and we do jobs that should've been taken over by robots years ago, just so we can swagger around on a testosterone high. It's crazy."

Tony Raglan was a man of surprises – the most masculine-looking of men, more than capable of holding his own on the rugby pitch or in a bar room brawl, yet he'd looked at the culture that was coming to be known as "toxic masculinity", and calmly, quietly, at no apparent personal cost, turned and walked away from it.

Good old Tony... I turned, and slowly began to walk back to the crash scene. They might need me. They might have got the lads out by now. There might be something I could do.

# RAGNAROK

*Dammit.* She"d seen me – that wasn't supposed to happen. What the hell had she even been doing out there, at that time of night – that time of morning? It was all so completely unfair. She shouldn't have been there. She shouldn't have seen me. But she had.

And now I'd have to kill her, when I hadn't planned it well enough, hadn't intended it. I had to risk screwing up, just because she'd bloody *seen* me. Because she'd been somewhere she shouldn't have been, at a time no decent person was meant to be out.

She'd been on the opposite side of the road, tottering back to her car after walking some young guy, maybe in his late twenties, up the path to one of the flats, but she'd seen me, staggering out of the alleyway that ran along the back of the opposite row of terraces, the row of terraces that served every sexual need you could imagine, at a price even an unsuccessful businessman would be willing to pay.

The businessman whose life I'd taken hadn't been unsuccessful. Hadn't been a man, in fact.

You had to ask yourself what kind of woman frequented a place like that, when she clearly wasn't on the game herself? No one decent, that's for sure.

Throttling the bitch with that stupid Scandi plait of hers had been particularly enjoyable. I liked strangling people. Liked getting up close and personal, liked feeling and smelling the change in them, from surprise to anxiety to blind terror. And I liked feeling the life flow out of them beneath my fingertips. I'd never used a person's plait before, but that was because I'd never killed someone who wore their hair that way before. I'd been surprised to find that hair didn't break easily.

And then I'd calmly unthreaded the black ribbon she'd had threaded through the braiding, and tied it round her neck, first slipping *Fehu*, the rune for wealth, onto it, in its wire-wrapped cage. *Fehu.* My signature - my explanation.

I would need to be more careful, next time. I would need to make sure there was no way I could possibly be seen. I had identified my next victim a week ago, before this killing, and I knew I knew I would have to vary my method. I couldn't strangle a second victim. I couldn't create a pattern, because patterns became paths, and paths lead to doors.

I had no wish to have anyone knock, knock knocking on my door over the deaths of people who needed to be put down, thank you.

And then there was the old woman. Damn her, I didn't want to kill her. It would make everything too complicated.

It was already complicated, the work I was engaged in. I was building a world, you see, a world in which everyone would feel happy, be prosperous, enjoy security. But that was a big ask, given the way the current world worked, the way it had worked for centuries. In order to effect a change of the magnitude I intended, the only acceptable sacrifice was blood.

Blood is the ultimate bargaining chip, the one that always finds favour with the gods. Think about it: Abel spilled blood upon the altar – not even the blood of something that was his to kill: he was a shepherd, which, in those days, would have meant he was tending someone else's flock. Probably Adam's, since we're talking about the time when, if not the entire human race, then at least the part of it that mattered to the Jews had only recently come into being. He killed a lamb that probably wasn't his, and God was pleased. Then Cain, an arable farmer, rocks up, with wheat he's grown, and God is furious – where's the blood? How very *dare* Cain not take a life in order to curry favour with the Lord?

So, Cain goes off, and spills his brother's blood, soaking the ground in sacrifice. And God doesn't just not punish him – he bans anyone else from ever punishing him! I mean, some theologians claim that Cain *was* punished, that he wanted to be killed, because it would have been seen as the only honourable thing to do after he'd killed his own brother, so God saying "Ah, no – not going to let that happen" was the worst punishment imaginable – but I don't see it. Cain gave God blood, and God saw that it was good. If it bleeds, it leads the gods to bless any and all endeavours.

Blood is in every foundation, on every cornerstone, the tribute and the plea offered at every new beginning.

Blood in, blood out.

I will build a peaceful world on the foundations of blood spilled by my own hand. Blood will buy everyone the equality years of negotiation and bloodless bargaining have failed to produce.

We kill things every day to further our own ends – animals, so that we may have meat, the health of the soil, so that we may have sufficient plant matter, unborn children, so that we need not be encumbered, our hopes and dreams, so that we may acquire a sufficient monetary standard of living.

All lives are not equal. By removing those that contribute to inequality, I'm simply balancing the scales.

## P.C. Feroc Hanson
## LB 599

"Feroc... Feroc... can you hear me? My name's Maddy, I'm a paramedic. If you can hear me, just open your eyes."

I blinked slowly, tasting something sour in my mouth, feeling like I was being slowly rocked to sleep, even as I struggled to wake. The darkness was so warm, so safe. The voice sounded as though it came from somewhere cold and dangerous and far away.

The light felt like fire, and I fought against the urge to cry out. I would *not* cry out, not while Tony might not make it. Not while he was hurting and afraid.

"That's it. That's good. Feroc? Feroc, stay with us. Come on – you can do this, Feroc."

My name was deafening on this woman's lips, her voice drawing me, ordering me, to let the light in.

I opened my eyes fully – and remembered, in a rushing howl of rage and fear and pain, why I hadn't wanted to.

"Tony!"

A low, soft moan, then a hissed growl, like something wild fighting its own death. Heavy breathing, and a deeper, more resonant growl. Something unnatural about it all. Something not quite human.

I turned my head, slowly – and saw sparks flying, a blurred outline of something standing over the still, silent body of the man I loved, a chainsaw in his hands.

I was deafened by my screams, and suddenly pinned by strange, strong arms. Something sharp bit down, piercing the skin of my forearm … and the darkness was given back to me in a sickening lurch. My last conscious gesture was to lay my hand on Tony's shoulder, gripping it with a gentle firmness that was becoming our trademark – it was this same gesture, this same gentleness, that had begun the love story that, I was certain, would end here.

As the darkness closed in, I heard a whisper from my lips:

"Odin, accept the souls of your faithful, fallen. Bragi, sing home these souls, whose time on Midgard is done."

## Inspector Bill Wyckham
## LB 81

The scream had me running without thinking, the way all screams have all coppers running. That's what it means to be a Blue, whatever service has claimed your life – you never get to walk when you hear a scream, not towards it, and certainly not away. And you never, ever, have the luxury of not hearing.

I must have run, time, even if only seconds, must have passed, but I would have sworn under oath that I had simply materialised by the Area Car, on the dying note of that bloody awful scream. Some things, you knew as soon as you experienced them you would never be able to forget – Feroc's scream was one of them.

I'd heard coppers scream before – it was rare, but, sometimes, human hellishness got through the shields of professionalism and experience. Sometimes, what you faced was so bad, it stopped you being you for a moment or several. But I'd never heard anyone, or anything, scream the way Feroc screamed. I couldn't tell you how I knew it was Feroc – I just *knew*. I wasn't even sure Tony's vocal range was capable of a scream. I imagined him bellowing, raging, howling – but I couldn't conceive of him screaming.

I rounded on the nearest paramedic, fear becoming rage.

"What the hell was that? Why was he screaming like that? What the hell did you do to him?"

To the eternal credit of both herself and her service, the medic heard me out, let me stop, panting and wild-eyed, before calmly responding.

"The younger officer – Feroc – came round and saw the fire crews cutting the driver free. I don't think he was fully aware, and, obviously, that's a frightening sight at the best of times."

I glanced into the car. "Why's he so quiet now? Is he okay? Are they going to be okay?"

"He passed out – shock. That's actually a good thing, it shields the brain from the worst impact of trauma. It makes emotional and mental recovery a lot easier. Sorry – excuse me." She hurried over to one of the fire crew, who'd gestured to her just as she was finishing her sentence. I heard the murmur of conversation, but not the words, saw her glance back at the wreck a couple of times, her eyes straying to Tony each time, drifting from him to the old lady in the Escort, then back to Tony.

I looked at the two men properly, for the first time since I'd arrived at the crash site.

I'd seen Tony Raglan asleep before – behind the wheel of the van on obbos, stretched out on the uncomfortable sofa in the break room when he'd had to work a double shift to save us being without a mobile unit during an outbreak of 'flu. Then, as now, he looked a lot younger, but still not quite at peace – a child in the grip of unpleasant dreams, yet dimly aware that he was dreaming, that there was no need to be afraid.

Feroc looked as though he'd just brought news from Marathon to Athens, and didn't have the strength for the return journey.

His face was completely blank, his mouth hung slackly open, and a trickle of blood was inching its way down his temple, where it had stained the roots of his dirty blond hair.

He needed a haircut – I'd have to remind him of the regulations, once this was over. I wasn't surprised Tony hadn't harried him about it – Tony had to be reminded to drop by the barber's, too. His hair was shorter than Feroc's, but somehow always managed to look the more unkempt. The only time his tawny, reddish-gold mop, shot through with the inevitable grey, didn't look as though it was about to leap off his head and run for the hills was when he was in Court. On those days, his hair was forced into a stylised submission, matching the way he looked in his dress uniform – unnatural, and uncomfortable, like a painting of a police officer.

The paramedic stepped back, a lightness in her gait. She raised fingers to her lips, and whistled, a single, shrill note that startled the seagulls, and had everyone turning to face her.

"Okay – can we clear the scene? The brigade are ready to bring the driver out."

A cheer went up, and, just beneath it, I heard stretcher legs clicking into place, light wheels and heavy boots on tarmac. I turned, and saw burly firemen bracing themselves against webbing straps, holding the crumpled metal of what had once been a top-flight BMW clear as paramedics knelt, ready to begin the delicate process of getting Tony Raglan's large, broken body clear of the wreckage. They knew what they were doing, what was needed. I saw the stretcher come into place behind them, saw a second team of medics hurrying round to the passenger side, a third waiting by the Escort. The two ambulances stood at a distance, their blue lights arcing through the air, brighter than the dawn.

Harry Beresford strolled over, taking in the scene."My lads have got a full diversion set up – we'll keep it in place until just before the rush hour. That'll be enough time to make site notes, get all the photographs and statements we need, and shouldn't piss Joe Public off too much. If the driver of the Escort pulls through -" he glared at the old woman as she was wheeled past on a stretcher, headed for a waiting ambulance - "I want to know what the bloody hell she thought she was playing at."

I nodded. "You and me both, Sergeant."

At that moment, my radio crackled. "Lima-Bravo Eight-One from Lima-Bravo, receiving?"

"Go ahead, Lima-Bravo." Beresford raised an enquiring eyebrow: it would have to be something serious, for Aimee Gardiner to interrupt me at this particular scene.

"Sorry, Sir, but there's been a body found – woman, IC1, late forties. Alleyway between numbers thirty-eight and forty, Haresfoot Way."

"Received, Lima-Bravo. Show me on way."

"Thank you, Sir." There was a pause, then, quieter: "How is everything there?"

"They're getting Tony out now – Feroc should've been in an ambulance ages ago, but the daft sod wouldn't let them near him until he knew Tony was alright. The other driver's already loaded up and on her way."

"Her? It was a woman driving, Sir?"

"Yes. Elderly lady. God knows what she was playing at. But Feroc and Tony are both clear – they're getting them into the ambulance now."

I heard the faint cheer from the other officers in the CAD room, and smiled. I loved being part of a team, part of a family. I loved that we were there for one another, that we cared what happened to one another.

My smile broadened as I remembered Raglan and some of the other lads introducing me to a Facebook page, UK Cop Humour – take the banter of your average nick, and multiply it by a social media presence in the thousands, all coppers, all wanting to kick back and let off some steam. It was glorious. It was home.

Feeling calmer and happier, at long last, I walked over to my car, and prepared to face the scene of the ending of a life.

# RAGNAROK

Claire Jakely. That had been her name, apparently. I was surprised how quickly she'd been reported – I suspected someone, most likely several someones, had found her before the ubiquitous "man walking his dog", but had not felt it prudent to report her death, and face having to explain just what, exactly, they themselves were doing in that vicinity, at that hour. Evidently, the old woman in the blue Ford Escort hadn't said anything. Perhaps she'd convinced herself she was seeing things, jumping at shadows. Perhaps she'd crashed her car and killed herself – a likely possibility, given the speed she'd been travelling at. Either way, it meant I didn't have to take her out of the equation, didn't have to change my plans to accommodate her. That was good. It meant I could relax, and focus on my next job.

I sat up as the news continued, reporting a crash on the Bascule Bridge... between a blue Ford Escort, and a police car. There was a reference to the "elderly female driver" of the Escort. Critical condition, as was the driver of the police car. His colleague was "serious but stable."

It couldn't be a coincidence. There simply couldn't have been two old ladies, both driving blue Escorts, both behaving in a manner likely to attract police attention, on the same stretch of road at the same time.

I could see, in my mind's eye, how the crash had played out. My old dear was flying along in a panic, PC Plod decided to give chase – the bridge came up to a let a ship through, old dear didn't stop, PC Plod tried to be a hero.

I got up, switched off the radio, and went through to the kitchen, to begin the mundane motions of making coffee: spoon beans into cup, brown spilling over white. Listen as the kettle huffs and puffs itself to a steamy cataclysm. Wait. Pour hot, not boiling, water over the dark brown beans in the white cup. Stir. Splash in creamy whiteness. Stir. Spoon in pure, crystallised whiteness. Stir, stir, stir. Clink of thin metal spoon against thick china mug. Pick up the mug, feel its weight. Take white mug to red armchair on blacklegging'd legs, grey socks on cream carpet. Sit.

I drank my coffee, and thought about the old lady. I hoped she died – it would make things neat, tidy. I couldn't stand mess. It was too quiet – I put my coffee down on a coaster, on the side table, and switched the radio back on. The news had finished: some eighties pop song was bouncing around.

Good morning, Great Britain.

I picked up my coffee, and drank it as the sun finally fought its way through the gap in my living room curtains.

## P.C. Leah Black
## LB 348

The body in the alleyway at Haresfoot Way didn't make any kind of sense.

 I'd pulled the car up, directly in front of number thirty-eight, a house we all had a lot of reason to be suspicious of, but not enough evidence to be kicking in doors on the strength of, and got out, closely followed by Robbie Graves. It was his first death scene as first-on, and my first that wasn't a suicide or a road accident. Well, it wasn't *thought* this one was suicide or accident, at least, unless you take the view that murder is simply a result of the accident of annoying the wrong person at the wrong time.

 A stocky, middle-aged man with a lean, wolfish dog – Husky, I guessed, but I wasn't great with mutts – waved from the mouth of the alley, while his dog whined and twirled on the end of its rope.

 "She's just down there, officers. Sort of off to the left, right at the other end. Quinn – enough!" The dog's ears went back, but it didn't stop the whining – or the twirling. "Quinn!" A short, sharp tug on the leash, and the dog flopped theatrically to the ground with a long, grouchy moan.  I decided I liked this guy – he was the kind of dog owner who didn't let his pet cause problems, and, from the flimsy mint-green plastic I could see bundled into a coat pocket, he was the kind who didn't leave traces of them for other people to deal with. He also, it seemed, treated  his dog as what it was – an animal, capable of causing harm, in need of discipline, rather than a furry baby.

 He smiled as the dog began to whine, pawing at the ground and looking as though it was thinking of getting up. "Sorry – d'you mind if I get on? Quinn doesn't like standing still."

 "If we could just take your address, sir?"

 "Of course – Quinn, settle." The man – Rohan Ireland – turned out to live in the next street. I smiled.

 "I'll walk you back. You know what to do, Robbie? The Inspector's on his way, anyway."

 Robbie swallowed, and nodded. "I'll be fine." He paused. "The

Inspector? Wyckham?"

"We have another Inspector on this shift?"

"But wasn't he -"

"He was. And now he's coming here. So be nice."

"Right."

The dog stopped whining as soon as his master started walking. I didn't care for dogs, but I had to admit, this one moved well, a steady, unhurried clip, head straight, ears up and forward, tail at half-mast. He didn't appear to pull, didn't appear to want to bother anything. He was growing on me, apart from the earlier whining.

"Is that a Husky?" I asked, by way of an ice-breaker.

"No – Anglo Wulfdog. Huskies typically have lighter, softer fur, they're broader, and their faces are slightly more rounded. Plus they'll have masks."

I'd stopped listening on the third syllable. "That's a *wolf*? As in, a wild wolf?"

Rohan Ireland laughed. "Only about 23%. The minimum required for DEFRA registration is 25%."

"So...one of his parents was a wolf?"

"His sire was 50% wolf, 50% dog. His mother was all dog, or as much dog as any canine ever really can be. She was maybe 5% wolf, something like that. Her mother was a Husky/Malamute mix, her sire was a German Shepherd. I wouldn't keep an actual wolf as a pet, or even a full hybrid – lot of work, lot of difficulties. Not really house animals."

"And this one is?" I wasn't convinced. Rohan smiled.

"Yes. Apart from the shedding and the insistence on digging up the linoleum to see if there might be more food under it after every meal. Oh, and taking melon rinds out of the bin, and trying to snatch melon from the counter while you're cutting it – he likes melon."

The dog glanced back, as though enquiring as to whether the mention of melon meant some was in the offing. Realising this wasn't the case, he returned to his focused, straight-ahead stare, a stare I recognised from times I'd been in the Area Car with Tony Raglan, and had caught his face while he was driving. His eyes, like this dog's, were always focused on some point in the near distance.

Abruptly, the dog paused, glanced back, and, at a flick of the leash, turned into a small courtyard in front of a terraced house. I'd imagined somewhere bigger, though I don't know why – I knew what the houses round here were like, after all.

"Here we are", Rohan Ireland said, unnecessarily, rummaging for a key and unlocking the front door. "Quinn – wait." He stepped past the dog, seeming to deliberately nudge its shoulder. The dog didn't protest, just turned and glanced at me.

I glanced at Rohan, who nodded. I stepped through, careful not to touch the dog.

"Quinn – house." The dog trotted in, waited for Rohan to take its leash off, and made a beeline for a pile of blankets, settling into a busy frenzy of rucking them about on the floor.

Rohan Ireland sat down in a white wicker armchair. I took the leather sofa across from him, and pulled out my notebook. "If you could just talk me through what happened, how you came to find the body."

"Sure. I take Quinn out at the same time every morning – about half five. He gets up around half four, I let him out into the yard, out the back, then he has his breakfast, I have a cup of coffee, and we're out soon afterwards. It takes a bit of time for him to calm down enough for me to allow him to go out – we don't have nice things if we're fussing, do we, Quinn?"

Quinn glanced up from his pile of blankets, seeming for all the world to grin at Rohan, before wagging his tail a couple of times, and stretching out to sleep.

"Anyway, it's usually somewhere between five and half past that we're out – Quinn gets nervous if there's too many people, so it's better for him to go out first thing, before the hoards descend." Rohan Ireland smiled in the dog's direction, and I wondered if I needed to revise my opinion of him as not being someone who thought their pets were actually human.

"So, as I was saying, we went out. We always walk the same route – Quinn likes his routine: we go down the road here, round the corner by the shop, down the hill, into town at the far end. We circle back around, come back along the access roads, and finally cut through the alleyway in Haresfoot, before heading along home."

I considered my next question carefully. "Mr. Ireland...do you...are you..."

"Do I know that number thirty-eight Haresfoot Way is a brothel? Yes, officer – Quinn's startled more than a few early-morning reprobates hurrying away. It wasn't hard to imagine what they'd been up to."

"But you've not been there yourself? Into the property, I mean?"

"No. I'd have no reason to."

"Why's that?"

"I don't do drugs, and I'm asexual, officer. I *am* married, before you start making the usual mis-connection and assume that I'm actually trying to tell you I'm a celibate gay man."

As if on cue, a stair tread creaked, and a light, female voice called through: "Ro? Is that you? Who're you talking to?" Footsteps, more creaking, and then a woman appeared, tall and lean, her tawny hair worn in a neat bob. She had obviously just got up – her hair was slightly tousled, and she was tugging an emerald-green silk robe closed over white pyjamas. "Oh. Police. Is everything – Quinn didn't -"

"It's alright, Pat. Quinn found a body. Some poor woman...dead, up behind that house on Haresfoot."

"It was bound to happen, all the things that go on there." Pat, I could tell, disapproved.

"Now, Pat – no one deserves to be killed because of the way they choose to spend their time, do they?"

"I suppose not." She stalked through into the kitchen, all feline grace. The dog whined, ears back. "Hush, Quinn. You've had everything for this morning." She didn't even glance back. I heard the kettle boiling, and took advantage of the sound.

"Your wife -"

"Is also asexual. In Pat's case, she's also aromantic. I am not – I enjoy romance, doing romantic things, the fun of it. But I respect that that isn't Pat's way. Intellectually, we're about as compatible as two human beings can be – we often joke that we're actually the same person, just of the opposite sex. We get along perfectly."

There was a clattering at the door, and the dog began to moan furiously. A white, fluffy head shoved itself angrily through a cat flap I hadn't noticed before, and a large white cat with bright blue eyes stropped into the room, raaahhhing loudly. It paused, and turned, slowly, to face me.

And hissed.

"Wraith! Be nice to guests, please." Pat came through from the kitchen, and set a mug of coffee down on a low table beside a rocking chair that the cat was already making a beeline for. "Do either of you want anything? Tea? Coffee? Ro?"

"Coffee'd be great. Officer?"

"No, thank you. If you could talk me through how you came upon the body?"

Pat strolled back to the kitchen. The cat blinked at me from the rocking chair. The dog moaned, and folded its nose under its tail.

"Well, as I say, it was Quinn, really – he lunged forward, and I assumed he'd seen something on the floor he thought he could eat – he has a sensitive stomach, so, of course, I stepped in front of him to try and keep him from getting whatever it was, and...well...I...I trod on her. On her fingers, I think."

"That must have been a shock."

"I didn't process what it was, not at first. Of course, poor Quinn set up a howl...he was very distressed...I looked down and...well, it became obvious what had happened." He paused, glancing up as his wife returned and handed him a mug of coffee. "Thanks. Ahh, that's better. Anyway, I always have my mobile on me when I go out, so I called you lot, and, well, here we are."

"Quite. Did you see anything? Anyone around?"

"I'm afraid not, sadly."

"That's okay – it was early. Although...I think I may have seen a young woman – at least I think it was a woman – going into a house a couple of doors along, with a Staffy."

"When you say 'a couple of doors along...'"

38

"Heading this way. Towards the junction with Mycroft Avenue."
Rohan Ireland named the street we were currently on. I nodded,
and made a note. "But you didn't get much of a look?"
"No, as I say, I'd just reached the end of the alley – I was waiting
for you – and she was going back into her house."
"This would be forty-two, forty-four?"
"Not forty-two. She would have been closer. Forty-four,
probably."
"Okay, that's helpful. Thanks. Are you in, during the day, if we
need to contact you?"
"Yes. I work from home. My wife works in Waterstone's in town."
"And what is it you do?"
"I'm a PR consultant."
That *was* a surprise – he looked more like an accountant. "Any
brands I might have heard of?" I smiled, making it clear this
wasn't an official question. He laughed, a little awkwardly. "Ah,
not really. It's...financial services PR. When the banks cock up -"
"They call you."
"Exactly, yes."
So, he was an accountant, after all. I wasn't usually wrong about
people.
 I got up. "Well, thank you for your time. We'll be in touch if
there's anything else."
"Of course."
I showed myself out, walking past the glaring cat. Pat had elected
to perch on the coffee table. It was pretty clear how the pecking
order went here, anyway. Cat, Pat, Rohan, dog.

 When I arrived back at the scene, Wyckham was already there, as
were SOCO and CID – I spotted the DI, Roscoe, and his DC, Tam
Freud. The pathologist was just pulling up – as were the Press. At
a nod from Inspector Wyckham, I headed over to the cordon, to
try and keep the vultures on their authorised perches.

### DI Mark Roscoe

I pulled on the blue plastic suit that SOCO would murder *me* if I didn't wear, and joined Tam, who was already suited, booted, and on-scene, crouched over the body, talking to the pathologist, Neil Anderson.

"What's that?" I pointed to a wooden disc, tied to the victim's wrist by a length of black ribbon – to judge by the blonde hairs, the ribbon had been yanked from her plait.

Anderson glanced up. "I'm not sure. It looks like a Norse runemark, but I wouldn't know which one it was, or what it meant, I'm afraid."

"Runemark? Like, runes? That people use for divination?"

"Do they? Well, I suppose so. Of course, runic is simply a language, albeit a written one. This is one letter of an alphabetic system. I couldn't tell you which letter, though."

My ears had pricked up at the first mention of *runemark.*

"People do use them as a form of divination. Like tarot cards."

People, I thought, like Tony Raglan. He should still be on shift, just about.

"I might know someone who can tell us more about this runemark," I said, nodding at the disc. Neil Anderson looked up, his expression showing pleased surprise. "Really? That would be fascinating. An academic, is he?"

"No", I smiled. "A copper. A queer, Pagan copper."

"Heathen." The correction came from Tam Freud. I glanced at her. "There's a difference?"

"Oh, yes!" Neil gushed. "I was very interested, in my youth, in the non-Abrahamic religions, including Paganism – which is much more of a nature-based, reflective practice – and Heathenry, which tends to focus its devotions on the Norse pantheon, and be much more about action than thought." He paused. "I'm surprised to hear there are Queer Heathens, though – it's a very masculine way of living, Heathenry. A man's religion."

Tam Freud sighed. "Tony Raglan isn't Queer. He's just gay. Sir."

"Aren't they the same thing?"

"No, Sir. 'Queer' refers to someone who deliberately stands outside of the heteronormative social structure, often as a form of political statement, usually in a very visible way. Some gay and lesbian people are also Queer, but a lot of them – like Tony – are happy with the system they're living in, they're just not heterosexual. They don't want to be seen as "other" - they just want to live a regular life, loving whomever they happen to love."

"Well, whatever he is or he isn't, Tony Raglan will know about this rune?"

"I would assume so, yes."

"Sir -"

I spun round. A WPC I vaguely recognised from around the nick was standing there, looking anxiously awkward.

"What is it?"

"About Tony Raglan, Sir... Lima-Bravo One was involved in a serious POL-AC earlier this morning, on the Bascule bridge. Tony and Feroc are in hospital. Sir."

*Not again. It couldn't be happening again.*

My mind flashed back to that scene, so many months ago, now – two years or more, it had to be, the panicked, restless crowd outside the Heart of Darkness, and Tony Raglan, gutshot and pale, being carried out on a stretcher. He must be close to sixteen, seventeen stone, yet the medics carried him as though he were a child. And Feroc, not yet Tony Raglan's lover, but realising that might be his future, sitting in stunned silence, staring at the blood on the tiles, Bill Wyckham's hand on his shoulder. That had happened because of a POL-AC. It couldn't be happening again. It just couldn't.

"What happened?"

"I'm not sure, Sir. All I know is, they were hit while in pursuit -"

"*They* were hit? The Area Car? Not the suspect vehicle?"

"I believe so, Sir, yes."

That couldn't be right. There was no way you could ram a police car while it was in pursuit – especially not when Tony Raglan was driving.

"Raphael's?" I barked. The WPC – I remembered, belatedly, we

weren't meant to call them that these days – nodded, mutely.
"Tam! Get a photo of that rune thing – send it to my phone.
Bloody Raglan had better be able to bloody talk. I swear he's done
this deliberately, just to annoy me." I was jog-trotting as I spoke,
car keys swinging from my fingertips. If he was unconscious, or
non-verbal, I would happily wring Tony Raglan's neck. He
couldn't have picked a worse time to screw up, yet again, in quite
spectacular fashion.
 Suddenly, something struck me: the accident had happened on the
Bascule bridge – and Haresfoot Way ran on to London Road,
which led to the bridge. What if the driver Tony had been
pursuing had been our killer, fleeing the scene?
I turned round. "Constable!" Both Tam and the uniformed officer
glanced up. I nodded at the latter. "You. What about the driver of
the suspect car?"
"I...I think they're in hospital too, Sir."
"Good."
I might have this all wrapped up before breakfast. How do you
like your eggs? I like mine with a collar, if possible.

## Sonia

I'd literally just stepped onto the ward when I saw Tony Raglan's name on the surgery board.

"You are an absolute cretin, Raglan," I muttered. Patients would be arriving for elective surgeries in less than an hour, and I would probably be the person assigned to telling them those surgeries weren't happening this morning, and perhaps not today. Then I saw Feroc Hanson's name.

"Mags!" The senior charge nurse paused. "Tony Raglan, Feroc Hanson – what happened?"

"A car crash. Quite a serious state of affairs. They had to have the brigade there for over an hour. Tony Raglan has cracked ribs and a possibly grazed lung, as well as a fractured arm, Feroc Hanson has pelvic injuries. We're really quite worried about him."

"He's going to make it, though?"

"He's young and fit, that will be in his favour."

I shook my head, trying to imagine Tony wanting to carry on if Feroc died. I couldn't see it – those two were so right for one another, they may as well have been two halves of the same person.

I'd never gone for that "other half" stuff before – it had always made me angry, the idea that someone would be incomplete without another person, but, with Tony and Feroc, it made sense. They *wouldn't* be whole without each other. Feroc was too naïve, and Tony was too... cynical wasn't right, but there was something missing in the way he interacted with the world, and the way he allowed it to interact with him. Something that Feroc had, but Tony didn't.

"Are they in theatre now?"

"Yes. I'm sure you have enough to do without worrying about those two." Her voice radiated disapproval. I felt my hackles rise – twenty years ago, when my sister Eva had ended up in hospital with anorexia, the doctors and nurses had radiated that exact same disapproval towards and about her. The disapproval that said: You chose a lifestyle I'll never agree with, so I have the right to treat you like crap because of it. I have the right to let my distaste for what you are and how you live impact on my judgement as a medical professional. I have the right to decide you're not worthy of concern, of compassion.

In Eva's case, they'd had the right to drive a young woman to suicide.

"Oh, I've got plenty to do, but they're Blues – it's different, isn't it?"

Mags snorted, a thoroughly equine sound. "I don't know what the world's coming to, letting people like that wear a uniform."

"People like what, nurse? People who'll put their lives on the line, over and over again, for scum who don't give a tup'ny damn? People who'll go out in all weathers, with a smile on their face? People who'll sit up all night, watching a house where a kiddy-fiddler *might* be living, because there's a ghost of a chance they can stop him messing some poor kid's life up? People who see the very worst humanity is capable of, and carry on anyway? Carry on caring, carry on helping, carry on serving?"

The man who'd come up behind me radiated anger. His eyes blazed with it.

"I need to speak to Tony Raglan."

"You'll have to wait – he's in theatre right now, and he won't be able to talk to you until late this afternoon, at the very earliest."

The man dropped himself into a plastic chair. "Then I'll wait." He took out a mobile, and tapped in a number. "Tam? Roscoe. Take over the reins, would you? I'm going to be at the hospital all day, looks like. Raglan's got himself booked in for an op, apparently -" the man gave a bark of laughter "- no, not *the* op. God, can you imagine Tony Raglan in a twinset and pearls?" More laughter. I fought down a smile. "Oh, god, Tam – I'll never get that image out of my head, now! You little witch!" He hung up, chuckling. Mags stalked off, radiating rage.

"What did she say?"

The man – I remembered his face, now, a Detective Inspector from Lothing – raised an eyebrow. "Tony Raglan in one of those negligee things, sprawled on a bed while Feroc feeds him grapes."

"Ewww!!! No offence, but that's just wrong!"

"I know. I don't even think Raglan knows what a grape *is*. Or a negligee, come to that."

I giggled, eyes bright with laughter. A couple of medical students stared at me, probably wondering if I were an escaped psychiatric patient.

"He's got to be the most unlikely gay man ever, really, hasn't he?"

"Oh, for sure. Tony Raglan is living proof that 'gay' isn't just a lifestyle or culture."

"Has he ever been part of the gay scene?"

"I can't imagine it, somehow. A guy like Raglan, in a gay bar? It's like trying to imagine a Miss World contestant working construction."

I stopped laughing, with a real effort of will. "You're really going to stay here all day?"

"Yep. I really need to speak to Raglan."

"Can I ask what it's about?"

"Something that was found at a crime scene. Something he'll know about."

"A symbol?"

"Yeah."

"Why not just Google it?"

"Because I want to hear from someone who's worked with the symbol, not just someone who's theorising about it."

A doctor stormed into the corridor, a tightly constructed tower of barely suppressed irritation.

"Tony Raglan is out of surgery. And he's already coming round." The Detective Inspector looked confused. "Surely that's a good thing, though?"

"No", I shook my head, getting in before the doctor could bellow his indignation. "It means the information we had on file for Tony Raglan, regarding his weight, was wrong. It means, since that information was given to a doctor from this hospital six months ago, when he conducted your nick's physicals, that Tony Raglan lied."

"Maybe he didn't lie – I mean, I know my weight varies, no matter what I eat, or how much I exercise -"

The doctor was shaking his head so hard, I thought it might explode. "Our formulas are based on a weight *range*. To allow for natural fluctuations, inaccuracies in equipment, that sort of thing. We were lied to, and this man could have died for the sake of, of – *vanity!*"

The doctor stormed off, slamming through the door at the end of the corridor.

"So, " the Detective Inspector smiled. "Can I see him now?"

I sighed. "I suppose so. But he'll probably be groggy." I turned to a final year medical student, who was looking terrified. I had a feeling she was supposed to have followed the doc, but had judged it safer to keep out of his way. "Do you know which bed Tony Raglan's in?"

"Private room – room three."

"Cheers. Come on, then – two minutes, though. You show him your symbol, you wish him well, you leave."

"Gotcha."

We headed into the maze of corridors that regularly brought us nurses hopelessly lost patients and family members, not to mention new members of staff. Finally, the corridor widened, one entire side becoming windows that looked out over the landscaped gardens to the rear of the building. We stepped into a lift, and went up a floor, to the corridor where we kept four large, en-suite rooms, for patients who either needed frequent personal care, and were aware enough to be embarrassed, needed a lot of medical equipment, or who, if neither of the previous two groups were in occupation, we simply liked enough, and expected to be with us long enough.

 Room one was occupied by a teenager, a wheelchair user who'd fallen from her horse during a riding for the disabled session. She had a private room because it enabled her to have her chair near by, which would, we hoped, encourage her to try and get up and about, which, in turn, would speed the healing process.  Room two was home to a schizophrenic who hadn't been able to settle on the psychiatric ward – he'd become convinced that the other patients were vampires, members of something he called the Sanguine Court, and were waiting until nightfall to rise and murder him. He'd tried to get in first, attacking a young man who'd been admitted after a little bout of taking an energy drink's advertising a little too seriously, and then going for a harmless-looking middle aged woman, whose arms were thickly wrapped with bandages, to hide the marks left by the bread knife she'd tried to cut away the pain with.

 I opened the door to room three, and bit my lip. Tony Raglan looked awful, and not just because of the vivid stitching and bruising. He looked as though his very soul had been torn apart.

"Hey," it came out as a whisper. Tony didn't move. We stepped closer to the bed. "Tony?"

He opened one swollen eye, moaning in pain. "Sonia. Guv." He tried to smile. The Detective Inspector sat down on one of the two chairs in the room, turning it to face the bed.

"There's a very unhappy doctor out there, Raglan. Seems you lied to someone, at some point."

"Hunh?" it was a sound, not a word.

"Never mind. Can you see okay?"

"Uh. Uh-huh." A deep, shuddering breath, an effort. "Yeah. Bit blurry, thas all."

"Good." The Detective Inspector – Roscoe – scrolled through his phone, and held it close to the one eye Tony had open. "Recognise it?"

"Yeah. *Fehu.*"

"What's it mean?"

"Means lotta things, Guv." I saw a flash of annoyance cross Tony's eyes – well, the one that was open, anyway – and he took another shaky breath. "Wealth." It was an effort, but his speech was less slurred, now. "Not always...money, though. Spiritual, sometimes. Or that you'll get good luck. New prospects." He blinked, and I thought I saw the glassy film of tears. He must be in a hell of a lot of pain.

Roscoe continued. "What would it mean if this were left at a crime scene? On a body, say?"

He glanced at me, a warning. I nodded in understanding.

Tony swallowed, once, twice. He took a painful breath. "I'd say there's a killer...going after...people he thinks are mor...mor...moral...morally bank...rupt. Guv." Sweat was beading on Tony's forehead, and the tears were becoming real. I stepped between Roscoe and the bed.

"That's enough now."

"Yes. It is. Thank you. Get well, Tony."

But Tony Raglan was already asleep.

### DI Mark Roscoe

As soon as we were outside Tony Raglan's hospital room, I turned to the nurse.

"The driver – the other driver who was involved in the accident. Is he here?"

She smiled. "Oh, yes. *She's* here. Edna. Shall I take you to her?"

My mind was reeling. She? A woman? And Edna – that was an *old* woman's name, wasn't it? This couldn't be right.

"You're sure this Edna is the driver involved in the accident that Tony and Feroc were involved in?"

"Yes. Definitely. She came round, briefly, in the ambulance, and was very concerned about 'those poor police officers.'"

I shook my head. None of this made sense. An *old woman* triggering a police pursuit? I couldn't even remember the last time I'd come across that, let alone a pursuit going at the kind of speeds that landed people in hospital, seriously injured. "You're certain?"

"Yes – I can take you to her, if it helps. Trust me, we were as stunned as you are – she seems such a harmless little thing."

I felt my hopes of an early arrest run away like sand through an upturned hourglass. I didn't need Raglan's rune reading skills to see press conferences in my future.

I *hated* press conferences.

"Yes, I think that's probably a good idea."

"This way, then." I followed the nurse.

"She didn't need surgery, then?"

"No – she was in shock, and her leg and arm were broken. She'll be in a wheelchair for a while, certainly, and I somehow doubt she'll be driving again any time soon, but she wasn't seriously hurt. A few cuts and bruises."

It was always the way. The people who caused all the mayhem walked away more or less scot-free, ninety-nine percent of the time, while everyone else bled out, suffered, cried, died, because of their actions or inaction.

I followed the nurse – I knew her name, I was sure of it, it was on the very tip of my tongue – onto the geriatrics' ward. There, in the third bed along on the right hand side, a thin, sparrow-like woman sat up in bed, a fretful old man at her side, clasping her hand. She had a pink fluffy dressing gown on, and a red and purple streaked face peered up from beneath a plume of ash-white hair.

The old man turned around, his eyes becoming anxious as he saw me. I took out my warrant card, an automatic gesture of reassurance.

"It's alright, sir. I'm with the police. Detective Inspector Roscoe. Are you the lady's husband?"

"Yes. My Edna, she didn't mean no 'arm. It was an accident, that's all!" His voice quivered, a high pitched wail of fearful protection. His wife patted his hand. "It's all right, Freddy. They'll need to talk to me about it, all the same. I was driving too fast. And if I hadn't been..." the smile left her eyes, and her lips trembled. "Well, those poor men wouldn't have been hurt. I don't think they'll be able to repair the police car, will they?"

"I'm afraid not, no."

"Will he get into trouble over that? The policeman who was driving, I mean? I wouldn't want someone to get in trouble because of me."

She sounded so sweet, so helplessly concerned. I bet she'd never had so much as a parking ticket in her life, before today.

"No, he won't. It's quite clear he acted in the way he felt was best. He wanted to stop your car going over the bridge."

"My Edna could've died?" Fred was panicky now, casting around for some kind of reassurance. "No one told me she could've died!"

"But I didn't, did I, Freddy? I'm right here, aren't I?"

"But you could've gone off the bridge! You could've died! What would I have done without you? What would I have told Sandra?"

"Sandra?" I glanced at the nurse, suddenly remembering her name: Sonia. Of course, it sounded like the name I'd just heard, that's what had brought it back.

"My daughter." Edna offered, trying to smile again. "She should be home from work by now. Oh, she'll be ever so worried if she can't get hold of us when she rings. She always rings after lunch. She works nights, you see, and she wakes up about half-past one, has her dinner, and starts getting on with things. Well, I suppose it's breakfast for her, really. I wouldn't've been there if she didn't work nights, see? I'd had to pick my grandson up, Tommy – he works casual shifts doing backstage work at the theatre. Days and nights, that is. He was working nights, same as his mum. If Sandra'd married a decent man, if she'd gone to university, like her teachers said she should –"

"Shhhh...don't you go upsetting yourself, Edna. You don't want to get poorly, do you?" Fred turned to me. "Like she says – if Sandra hadn't been working, she'd've picked Tom up, and none of this would've happened. I don't drive, see." He tapped his eye. "Glaucoma. Don't see well enough. It ain't right, them stopping me driving. They shouldn't leave Edna having to do everything."

"Fred."

"Can I just ask, Edna – it is alright if I call you Edna, isn't it?" She nodded. "Okay, Edna – why was it that you were driving so fast? Do you remember?"

"Oh, yes, my dear – I saw the devil."

I blinked. "The devil?"

"Only, it surprised me a little bit, seeing that he was a woman, but I suppose he can be whatever he wants, when he's on the earth. I mean, he's got all that power, becoming a woman shouldn't be difficult. I saw a programme the other day, about men who want to become women. Some of them did look very nice, after they'd seen all the doctors and that. You wouldn't really have known. And there were girls becoming boys, too. But it would be easier for the devil, I expect.."

"So, how did you know this was the devil, Edna?"

She stared at me, unblinking. "Why, because he'd killed someone, officer. That's what the devil does. Bad things. Wicked things. Murder is very, very wicked."

"It is indeed. Can you describe the devil to me, Edna? The devil you saw."

"Well, that's the thing – other than knowing he was a woman, I didn't *see* him – I don't think you're allowed to. It's sort of like God, you mustn't see immortal things – but he *felt* evil. He felt like the devil, you know?"

"But you knew it was a woman?"

"Yes – he had woman's hair."

I sighed. So, we were looking for a man with long hair. I wondered how many of those Lothing had, at last count? It was probably at least a hundred, depending on the length of hair.

"So, you saw the devil – and you drove away?"

"Yes. That's why I was going so fast. I was frightened, you see. I've never done a wicked thing in my life – the devil shouldn't have been anywhere near me!"

"If it helps, I don't think -" I paused "I don't think the devil was there for you. There are some people, in a house on that street, who do bad things, quite a lot of bad things. I think the devil had come calling for them."

"So he won't try and find me?"

Sonia shook her head. "No. The police officer's right – the devil was after the bad people in that house. Not you. And besides, he can't come in here – we're protected by Saint Raphael."

"Oh, that *is* a relief!"

"Someone oughta phone Sandra." Fred, not wanting to lose his place in today's spotlight, had begun to fret again.

"I'll get an officer round to see her, bring her over here. What's her address?"

"Twenty-seven, Haresfoot Way. She lives there with my grandson, Tom. He's twenty-six, but they stay at home 'til all ages, these days."

"We'll pop round, let her know where you are, and that everything's okay. You say she normally gets up about one?"

"Yes – I don't know about him, though."

"That doesn't matter for now." I stood up, my heart heavy at the thought of having to track down a killer whose only description was "man with long hair, looked like the devil in drag."

In drag. That brought back the image of Tony Raglan as an early-nineties Pamela Anderson, and I turned away quickly, trying to hide the look that crossed my face.

"Well, that's it for now – take care, and I, or one of my officers, might check in later, okay? And someone will bring your daughter over."

"Thank you, officer. Do let me know how those two men are. The younger one seemed very upset – I think he was crying, at one point. Was it his Dad, in the car with him? He seemed very worried about him."

"They're very close, yes." It wasn't a lie.

"Oh, that poor boy. They are both going to be alright, aren't they? I'm so terribly sorry."

"I understand. And they're in good hands. I'm sure they'll be fine."
I walked out of the room hoping I hadn't just lied to an elderly lady who thought she'd seen a sex-changed devil. I hoped I hadn't lied to myself. I hoped Lothing wasn't about to lose two fine, brave, bright officers.

Hope, I remembered my childhood priest once saying, was the beginning of prayer. Well, I wasn't much of a one for praying, so I just let the hope ascend. If someone, or something, heard, and responded? So much the better. And if not? Well, no one knew I'd hoped so hard, did they? There was no harm done.

# RAGNAROK

I don't want you thinking I just stroll around, eyeing people up until I find a likely-looking victim. I'm not like that. It takes weeks for me to identify a potential kill, then a few more weeks before I'll actually commit the act.

Murder is like getting married: you don't rush into it, and most people fool around for a bit before they settle down.

Yes, I'd killed before – several times, in fact. But I'd never been caught, mainly because I know about forensics, and I don't draw blood. I'd started with poison – the common kinds people will forget about you buying, or that you can find around the place, in the kitchen or the hedgerow. Poison doesn't even require you to be there when your victim dies. For some people, that's its attraction. For me, it was why I left it – I like watching, feeling, the life ebb away from someone I've spent time and effort courting. Poison was too impersonal, too remote. I mean, you *could* choose to be there when your victim ingested the poison, if you used something you could control the timing of the dosing on, but then people would expect you to *do* things – administer first aid, call an ambulance, blah, blah, blah. And besides, you might leave fingerprints somewhere you shouldn't.

Fingerprints are a bugger if you don't think about them – but a walk in the park if you do. Take some caustic soda – the stuff you use to clean drains – and hold your fingertips in it for twenty minutes, *after* you've committed your crime, but before the police are aware. And for the love of all that's holy, *not* at the crime scene!

It will hurt. It will hurt like hell. It will make you cry and scream and swear and want to die. But it will break the fingerprint loops and whorls, which are what identify you. The reason you need to do it after you've committed your crime? No two people scar exactly alike, either.

If blackmail is your gig – and it's been mine a time or two – and you want to go the old-fashioned route, buy a random selection of books from charity shops – different genres from different shops, for preference – and make sure you only touch the cover when you buy them.

Get them home, and put on a pair of latex gloves. Tear out the blank pages that tend to lurk at the back of books, and use these as your letter page, cutting out words and phrases from the other books and pasting them on.

Envelope wise, buy a single, loose envelope, from a busy stationery department or general store. Make sure you wear gloves when you go to post it. The point of this is to ensure that you have materials which are likely to have several other fingerprints on them already. Yours, if they make it there at all, should get lost in the mix. The police, even with technology, aren't very good at hearing the signal through the noise.

Technology brings me on to a better way to commit blackmail: Go to a busy, urban area, somewhere which is unlikely to be covered by CCTV – rear corners of coffee shops, by the toilets, are good for this – and use their wi-fi to set up fake social media accounts – but make sure you use a believable name, especially on Facebook. Follow a whole bunch of random businesses, including your target business. (You should always target a business when engaging in blackmail – the risks of them calling the police are higher, but so are the potential rewards in terms of payouts.) Spend the first few weeks just posting generic stuff – updates on your day, social commentary, cute cat pictures, that kind of thing – and then, slowly, start working in some rumours about your target company. Don't go overboard – just say a little more each time, over a period of weeks. People will start to pick up on it, hopefully.

At the point that other people are talking about the rumours in significant numbers – you want at least a hundred people, spread out across the country, as it makes it harder to trace the original source – you message the company from a *second* fake profile, and tell them you can stop the rumours, but it's going to cost. Don't make your demand upfront – wait for them to ask.

The point of using free wi-fi in a busy area? The signal can only be traced to a building, not an individual device. And smartphones are so cheap, these days, that you can afford to use and throw, once your blackmail is successful.

But I left blackmail behind some years ago – it was fun, but I'm better at murder.

After bidding poison a fond farewell, I embraced the 'convenient accident' school of sudden death – some faulty brake lines here, an unseen piece of clutter on a staircase there – you can imagine the sort of thing. That was fun, and a challenge find new yet believable ways to end a life.   But it requires being around, being visible, potentially being noticed, long before you make your kill. And that's a risk I didn't care for, in the end.

So, like the young Lothario tiring of STDs and unplanned pregnancies, I grew up, and settled down with strangling the idle, undeserving rich. Undeserving of their wealth, that is: murder, they richly deserved, in my opinion, and I was only too happy to ensure they were paid in full.

I picked up one of the hundred blank wooden discs I'd brought for just over six pounds on Ebay, pre-drilled, and a marker pen from a pack I'd brought from Poundland, and inked in my next talisman. I did each working of *Fehu* individually – it's the height of folly to leave your signature lying around, after all.  Why a hundred? Was I planning to kill a hundred people? Maybe – there's nothing wrong with ambition, after all.

## PC Tony Raglan
## LB 265

The light was bright, but distant: I could see it, but even imagining reaching it was exhausting. I felt tired – not the good kind of tired you get after an honest day's work, or a gym session, but the bad kind, the killing kind. The kind that gets right into your bones, and makes it hard to breathe.

I had a feeling I'd been dreaming, but my head felt too fuzzy for dreaming to have taken place. I usually feel strangely clear-headed if I wake remembering a dream, and I didn't now. Yet I was certain I'd dreamt that I was talking to Mark Roscoe about the rune *Fehu* – he'd been given it by a dying priest, or something, and wanted to know what it meant. I'd told him it spoke of coming good fortune, wealth or success. I'd joked – or thought I'd joked – that he should start playing the lottery, and he'd looked me dead in the eye, and snarled that the lottery was strangling people, that it was murder to play it...

Feroc – where was Feroc? I reached out a hand, expecting to feel either the solid litheness of him, or the warmth he'd recently risen from, and instead touched cold metal.

And felt pain.

Something was wrong, somewhere. The picture had lost something in the painting. I forced myself to walk towards the light, forced myself to open my eyes into its blinding glare.

This wasn't my bed. It wasn't my room. It wasn't my house. And Feroc was nowhere in sight.

Feroc should be here. There shouldn't be a white light – that wasn't part of my death mythology – and, if this was the light of Valhalla, or somewhere that the Norse-believing dead are made welcome, I didn't want to endure it, to enter it, without Feroc.

My heart skipped a beat as I realised what this could mean – that Feroc had already gone before me. That he was waiting for me on the other side, terrified that I wouldn't make the leap. But how could I, if I didn't know for certain he was there? I couldn't risk leaving him.

"Feroc?" My voice sounded strange. It was lacking something. I tried again. "Feroc! Stop buggering about, man!" A rush of air, and the sudden sound of voices, none of them Feroc's.

"FEROC!" It wasn't a shout. It wasn't even a scream. It was a wild sound, a sound no human should be able to make, or should have to hear. And it was immediately smothered by desperate voices, questioning, pleading, calling the one to the other.

And Feroc wasn't there.

## Sonia

"Excuse me?"

I turned round, smiling at the anxious face of a student nurse. "Yes love?"

"The patient in room three? I … I think he's awake. He's not making a lot of sense, though – he keeps saying something about 'the rock'? He sounds quite out of it."

I shook my head, still smiling. "Describe 'out of it' for me – I'm not familiar with that particular medical term." She gave an awkward laugh. "Well... he's very distressed. He was screaming – I mean, loud enough that you could hear him clear down the corridor. About this rock, or whatever."

The rock? It didn't make sense – but something, a name, that might sound very like 'the rock', from the lips of someone strung out on meds, to the ears of people not familiar with it, did.

"Could it have been 'Feroc?'"

The student nurse frowned. "I suppose so, possibly. I mean, it sounds like 'the rock', which is what I thought he was saying. But 'feroc' isn't a word. Is it?"

I shook my head. "No. But it is a name. The name of his partner."

"Do we know where she is?"

"He. And he's in room four. I was going to talk to the doctor about moving them in together, as it happens – guess I'd better do that sooner rather than later. I'll check in and see Tony first."

"He's gay?"

"Yes – that's usually the meaning of a man having a male partner."

"I wouldn't't've known -"

"They don't go around with pink stars any more, you know."

"No, I -" She had the grace to blush. "I just thought, y'know... I know gay men, a few, anyway. You can sort of tell."

I laughed. "Well, when you see Tony Raglan and Feroc Hanson together, you can sort of tell then, too. Come on – let's go and calm him down, shall we?"

Together, we headed up to room three. The student nurse hadn't been wrong – I could hear Tony's howling as soon as the lift doors opened.

A doctor flung the door open. "What the hell's he screaming like this for, nurse?"

That was always the way with doctors – they expected those of us who were paid less, and, as they made a point of remarking, *educated* less, to know pretty much everything.

"Have you tried asking him?"

"Have you *heard* the racket he's making?!"

"Yes. I don't *think* I put that I was deaf, or hearing impaired, on my application form. Try talking to him."

"Over that cacophony!"

I sighed, and pushed past the doctor, into the room. Poor guys – they really couldn't handle emotions. Or pain. Or distress. Or anything they couldn't medicate away immediately, or preferably remove at scalpel-point.

I stepped into the room, and the small crowd by the bed parted like the Red Sea when it copped a load of Moses. I stepped up to the bed, and laid a hand on Tony's shoulder, gazing right down into his frightened, furious face.

"Tony." I spoke softly, barely above a whisper, and I timed it to the moment he had to draw breath to scream again. He started choking, but managed to turn and look at me.

"You know who I am, don't you, Tony?" My voice was still soft, a lullaby. He gulped, spluttered, gagged, frothed at the mouth a bit, took a few shaky breaths, and finally spoke.

"Sonia."

"Good lad. Now, you're to hush that noise – you're upsetting the poor doctors. They don't know what to do with you."

"Feroc – where's Feroc?"

"He's in the room next door – I'm going to ask if he can be brought in here: there's room enough for two beds, and I think it will help him to see you, when he comes round."

"He's not conscious?" Tony's voice was panicky, becoming ragged and gruff where another person's would rise to falsetto.

"He was hurt pretty badly – it's best he stays out for as long as possible: it makes it more likely he'll heal properly."

"But he's going to get better? He's going to be alright?"
"Absolutely."
"How badly was he hurt?"
"He took a few serious knocks to some serious places. We thought, for a while, that he'd broken his pelvis, but it turned out he'd just chipped a bit of bone off his hip, knocked it out of whack a little. That's all sorted, but his ribcage and spleen are a bit of a mess."
"How? How was he hurt that bad? I mean, I'm not hurt that bad, I don't think, and he had an airbag, same as I did -"
"Yes, well, there's less of him to absorb the impact than there is of you," the doctor who'd been howling about Tony's screaming muttered. Everyone glanced between the two of them.
 "I'm right here, doc. And my hearing hasn't gone." But the fight wasn't there. Tony sounded... weary, rather than the mock-outraged I'd come to expect in response to statements like that.
I smiled, and spoke loudly enough for the doctor to hear, too: "It means there'll be something nice and soft for him to lay against, once he's well enough to go home. Better than these hard-angled coathangers that call themselves men. Spend so much time in the gym, or with their vegan-protein cookery books, I doubt they'd have the first idea how to get passionate." The room erupted into relieved laughter. The doctor glared.  I looked up, meeting his angry eyes.
 "So? Can I bring Feroc Hanson in here?"
He swung away, hand already on the door. "Do what you want."
I turned back to Tony. "I'll take that as a yes, then. One lover-boy coming through."
 Tony took my hand, a sudden, urgent gesture. "Sonia – you wouldn't lie to me, would you? Feroc's going to be okay, isn't he?"
"Of course he is." My face became serious. "We wouldn't be letting you see him if he wasn't."

## DI Mark Roscoe

It was almost 1am, and I was finally drifting off to sleep after too long spent doing too little on the internet, when my phone buzzed.

"Roscoe." I fully expected it to be a call to yet another crime scene, images of death and deprivation to mock my attempts at getting forty winks.

I was wrong – in the best way possible.

"I'm calling from St. Raphael's – I had a request to ring this number with updates on the progress of three of our patients, Tony Raglan, Feroc Hanson, and an Edna Pearce? Is that right?"

"Yes!" I snapped. "Are they okay? Tony and Feroc?"

"Yes, they're fine – Feroc Hanson regained consciousness a couple of hours ago. Tony Raglan's doing well, and Edna Pearce will be going home in the next couple of days, as soon as we can arrange for a carer to pop in an help her husband out."

I made a note of her surname. "Ok, that's great. Is she up to a formal interview, do you think? Obviously not right now – later tomorrow afternoon, say?"

"I think the doctor would prefer you waited until she was released. But you're welcome to come in and see her, and the two men. I can't give you her address, obviously."

"Of course not."

"Visiting hours are twelve until two, and four until eight."

I glanced at the LED display of my alarm clock. I wouldn't be going in first thing, that was for damn sure. "I'll swing by around twelve, then." I could head to the factory from the hospital, and run a late one. Flexi time was a wonderful thing. So was not having anyone at home to moan about it.

"That's fine. I'll leave a note to let the relevant doctors know you'll be by." There was a laugh in the voice. "I expect they'll want to keep an eye on you."

"Undoubtedly – can't allow rabble-rousing, can we?"

"Certainly not."

The call ended, I stared at my phone for a long moment, before deciding that a text, rather than a phone call, would probably be more appreciated by Bill Wyckham. After all, *he* did have a family to think about.

I also texted Tam Freud. I should've had a DS by now, but funding cuts meant promotion boards had been halted for the past two years in a row. Although, apparently, all that nonsense was "over", now – so maybe I could get my team back to full strength. Tam would be the first candidate I put forward, and I'd make damn sure she knew I wanted to keep her – she was a good officer, and I had no intention of losing her. She should have gone for the last board, but she hadn't had the confidence, although I personally felt sure she would have done, if the nightmare down at the Heart of Darkness hadn't happened. Something like that would knock anyone back.

But she'd come back fighting, and she definitely had the spunk for the job, now. I'd back her to the hilt, and she knew that. I'd never understood senior officers who didn't like women – women were often better at reading people, and would know the reality of a situation long before the blokes were even halfway towards suspecting that what we were hearing wasn't the whole truth. Women tended to be better at keeping hostage takers and would-be suicides calm. They tended to be better at getting confessions from female suspects, and evidence from traumatised victims. They cared more about making sure witnesses were on-side and up to scratch than male officers – we tended to focus too much on evidence and proof, forgetting, or not realising, that juries didn't understand forensics, and didn't care about minute details – they cared about people. It's why we had victim impact statements, after all.

I remembered Tony Raglan's comment, when those were first introduced:

"Great. So, if I get gunned down by some nutter -" he should probably take up with a crystal ball, with a gift like that for seeing the future - "it's going to matter less than some dopey chav getting knifed in a drugs dispute, because my parents aren't going to stand up there, sobbing for the cameras, and mewl on about how awful it is, how they don't know what they'll do without me?

It's going to matter less than some prat who's stupid enough to get into a car with a drunk driver, because I don't have an attractive girlfriend to dab her eyes and shake her head for the journos? It's out of order – Court's about facts, logic, objectivity – we can't start letting this rose-tinted crap in."

Bill Wyckham – he'd been a Sergeant then – had consoled him. "It's alright, Tony – we'll doll one of the WPCs up to look like a homely housewife, and she can sob about how you'd just proposed to her, and she was so looking forward to planning the wedding, and you were going to start trying for a baby, soon. We'll make it right for you."

Everyone had laughed – even Tony. It seemed impossible that he could have been gay, then, but I suppose he must have been. And now he had Feroc.

I wondered how people would react to a grieving boyfriend – and realised that the very fact that I was wondering that, and that I wasn't liking some of the thoughts I was having in response, was the answer to the question coppers in more metropolitan areas asked every year: Why do we need a bloody Pride parade? And, of course, the answer to every online bigot's howl - "Why don't we have Straight Pride?!"

Although, to be honest, I couldn't see Tony Raglan marching at Pride. I couldn't really see Feroc marching, though I could see him at some of the talks and events that Norwich tended to host around their main shindig. I could see him browsing the stalls, too. But Tony in the middle of all of that? It just didn't scan. It didn't seem right.

I wondered what that said about me – was I homophobic? I didn't think I was. Okay, other than Tony and Feroc, and Aimee Gardiner, I didn't know any openly gay people, but that wasn't because I avoided them – it was simply that, if other people at the nick were gay – and I'd be surprised if only three coppers out of an entire station were – they didn't say. I mean, if Feroc hadn't turned up, or if he hadn't been paired with Tony, maybe neither of them would have been openly gay, either. And I only knew about Aimee Gardiner because she'd knocked one of my lads back, very

64

gently, very professionally, and he'd been amazed that "dykes could be pretty, and nice, and, well, y'know – black." Everyone, including Aimee, had had a laugh about that. Billy Cassidy – what a plonker. Good copper, though. Still on my team, though he was angling for a transfer to a Yorkshire nick – he had a missus who wanted to get home.

My phone buzzed again. I smiled in surprise as I saw the number on caller ID.

"Bill – didn't think you'd still be up, mate. Yeah, good news all round. I'm going in to see them tomorrow, about lunch time – I won't be up for an early start tomorrow. What shift you on? Lates? Yeah, that's a nice idea, give them both a bit of company. Apparently they've moved Feroc in with Tony – he was kicking up merry hell, so they say. Tony – Feroc was unconscious at the time. The docs probably wished Tony was. Yeah, he's got a gob on him, alright. Anyway, I"ll probably still be at the factory when you get in tomorrow, so I'll see you then. Alright, mate, take care, yeah?"

I clicked the phone off, only for it to buzz again. "Tam – sorry, I was just talking to Bill Wyckham …."

# RAGNAROK

The important thing about murder, if you wish to be successful at it, is variation.

Vary your victims, as much as possible. Vary the time of day, the time of year, the location, the day of the week. Vary the places you dump the bodies, if you're not leaving them at the kill site.

Vary what vehicle you use, if any. Vary the way you present yourself. Vary the routes you take to the places where you search for your victims.

The one thing you should never vary, however, once you have found one that works, one that seems a natural extension of you, and of your reasons for killing, is your method of slaughter. Killers often form an intense bond, a kind of psychic link, with a particular way of killing, and such bonds and links, once forged, are not easily broken, and are rarely broken whilst keeping the individual in question whole, and mentally healthy.

A good killer is not a lunatic, is not numbered among the insane. My next victim was a male, in his mid-twenties, arrogant and opinionated, from his social media posts, and convinced that his inflated salary, paid for some species of brokerage work in the City of London, would protect him from all the evils of the world.

He thought evil was restricted to poverty, to deprivation: he hadn't counted on me. Wealth would draw my wrath upon you, rather than shielding you from me. I killed people because they were wealthy, and wealthy in a way that appalled me – that was my sole reason.

Every killer has a reason. No one simply wakes up one day, and thinks "Hmm, murder sounds fun." No, not even the teenagers who live their entire lives in a world of pretend slaughter. If they take to killing in the real world, they, like me, will have their own reasons. No one kills just for the thrill of it – whatever they or their psychiatrists might say.

I don't have a psychiatrist: I don't need one. I'm not crazy. And not being crazy was probably the most dangerous thing about me. Madness resulted in sloppiness, in mistakes, in acting without thinking.

Madness impaired decision making, and clouded the awareness of danger, and the proper assessment of risk.

Madness had probably been the downfall of many a promising killer.

I wasn't mad. But I was promising – and I most definitely was a killer.

## Inspector Bill Wyckham
## LB 81

I pulled up alongside the man who was walking, head down, lost in thought, and gave a short, sharp blast of my horn. The man jerked round, clearly startled.

"Wyckham – you nearly gave me a heart attack!"

"You heading to the hospital?"

"Yeah – you offering a lift?"

I nodded. "Get in. I'm afraid my driving isn't quite up to Tony Raglan's standards."

"Whose is?" Mark Roscoe sounded unfocused, inattentive, and not at all like the steel-bright, ever-alert DI I'd come to know. "What's up?"

"Nothing – why do you think something's up?"

I cut the engine as Roscoe buckled his seatbelt, making it clear we weren't going anywhere until I got the truth. I'd been up just long enough to have coffee, breakfast, and a shower – in that order – and get dressed: if Tony and Feroc hadn't ended up in the hospital, I wouldn't've been out of the house yet, and would be having at least four more cups of coffee before I even thought about a meal before I left for the late turn. I was not in the mood to be messed about.

"Come off it, Mark – you're miles away."

Mark Roscoe stroked his seatbelt, and stared out of the window. "This is so completely the wrong time for this..."

"Spit it out. Sometimes, you have to put on your big boy pants, and accept that there's never going to be a right time. What is it?" I laughed. "I won't kill you."

Mark Roscoe's gaze, when he finally looked at me, was terrifyingly bleak. "You might."

"For God's sake, man! Out with it!"

"There's a possibility...in a few months...six months, maybe, we're bringing together what we've got now, and working out whether it's safe to leave it, or if we'll need someone in sooner, that we'll need an undercover who can handle a freight job."

He paused, and I processed what he was telling me. "No. No way, Mark. God, man – Tony Raglan's been through enough! And what about Feroc? I'm not putting up with an officer with a hell of a lot of potential being sent off the deep end because his lover gets himself killed on some undercover job." I took a breath, fighting for composure. "Besides, I've already lost a copper to that world."

"Raglan's different. He's sound, upstairs. He's not going to go Looney Tunes on us, is he?"

"I'm not putting him at risk, Mark."

"And I'm not calling in the Yard on this. Or Norwich. My team have worked on this for almost a year, Bill -"

"Then let them work a bit harder. A bit longer."

"NO!" Mark Roscoe slammed his fist onto the dashboard, startling a passing pedestrian. I buzzed the window up. "No," he repeated, quieter this time. "We need someone on the inside. Someone on the wagons."

I looked at him, taking in every detail of his face, the visible and the invisible, listening to what he'd left unspoken, as well as what was being said.

"What's the job?"

He licked his lips, ducked his head. I saw him close his eyes, hard, as though against some inconvenient truth. When he opened them again, it was to stare straight at me.

"Guns."

My blood ran cold, and I could swear I felt my heart stop. My mind flashed back to that scene, two years ago, in the Heart of Darkness, to Tony's blood, too bright against the stark tiles of the floor. To the barmaid screaming – she was just a lass, twenty at most. To drinkers rushing outside. To those who'd stepped a little closer, only to be pushed back by the force of Feroc's wild, heartbroken energy, holding them off as effectively as an electric fence.

"No."

Mark Roscoe's gaze never left mine. "Don't you think that's up to Tony Raglan, Bill?"

"Hell, Mark – you know he'll say yes. He doesn't know how to refuse – he wants people to approve of him, so he'll do whatever

69

they ask!"
"I think you do him a disservice. As you identified, he has someone else to think about, now – someone who's existence we know of. Someone we expect him to consider before the rest of us."
"He'll always put the uniform first – that man's got 'copper' running through his veins. There's no way round that, Mark."
"I know you're worried, Bill, but you can't wrap him up in cotton wool and keep him safe forever. He'd only come to hate and resent you, if you did."
It was my turn to close my eyes, to try and keep from seeing the truth of Mark Roscoe's statement. Keeping Tony Raglan leashed, in order to keep him safe, was like buying a boat and never taking it out of the marina you chose to moor it in – you could do it, but that wasn't the point of a boat.
"I'll ask him."
"Thank you."
"You won't say a single word. You won't even look at him, until he's given me his answer."
"Agreed."
"Ideally, you won't even be in the room."
"I can go and get coffee."
"Good. That's sorted, then."
"As long as you accept his answer."
"I will do – he's my boy, always and forever, but he's not a child, a pet, or a possession – I have to accept that."
"I'll make things as safe as I can for him out there, Bill."
"I know you will." I paused. "He might not be well enough."
Mark Roscoe sighed. "I'm well aware of that. We'll cross that bridge when we come to it. If we come to it."
"If he's not well -"
"I know. I'll get the divisional surgeon's say so, before we run with Raglan on this."
"Right." I started the engine, and we drove to St. Raphael's in silence.
I remembered something I'd once heard Feroc say, that Tony had

greeted with derision – that several coppers had greeted with derision, actually. Feroc had said he didn't believe that people were 'good' or 'bad', only that they did helpful or harmful things. I think Tony had called him a bleeding heart liberal. Someone younger had called him a snowflake. Feroc hadn't even blinked.

He hadn't been going out with Tony, then – it hadn't been long after he'd started at Lothing – and I wondered if either of them remembered it. I wondered if they still talked about such differences of opinion.

I wasn't any kind of Christian, but I wanted there to be a hell, because I believed that people who did harm were bad, and deserved to be punished. And I wanted there to be a heaven, too, a place of peace for men like Tony Raglan, who gave of themselves day in, day out, without thinking about the consequences. A fire engine howled past us, and I wondered where it was headed, and what kind of risks its crew would be taking. I hoped they all made it home tonight. I hoped every Blue, wherever they were, whoever they served, made it home, this night and every night. Why should footballers and vainglorious celebrities be allowed to live in peaceful contentment, while all across the country – all across the world – men and women on a fraction of their salaries risked their lives and sanity day after day, night after night, often for very little thanks?

It wasn't right, and it wasn't fair.


"Just five minutes, please – they both need to rest."

I nodded. "Mark – go and get a couple of coffees, yeah?"

"No problem. I'll stick my head round the door for a minute or so once you've reassured yourself your boys are all in one piece. I've spoken to Tony already, briefly."

I watched Mark Roscoe walk away, and followed the nurse into the private room.

Hospital beds have a habit of being the most imposing thing in a room – there was no way anyone would describe Tony Raglan as slender, and yet he seemed frail and lost. Feroc, half Tony's size, looked like an orphaned child. But they were both smiling, if a little weakly. They were both at peace, the presence of each soothing and reassuring the other. And, strangely, the two beds didn't seem to crowd the room at all.

"Hey." I spoke low and light, a little above a whisper. Feroc struggled to open his eyes, Tony sat up, wincing a little, holding out a warning arm, tubes dangling from the back of his hand, a clear sign that he felt Feroc should take things a bit easy. I couldn't agree more.

"Guv. How's things at the factory?"

I grinned. "Well, the canteen food bill's halved – the brass are pleased about that, looks good when they report to the suits – and it's a lot quieter." I crossed to the single chair, and sat down. "Seriously, though, it's not right without you. Everyone's on edge, acting daft. I don't know what you do, but you seem to keep them calm. It goes to hell entirely when you're not around."

"Sorry, Guv."

"Yeah, well... they might have to learn to deal. Mark Roscoe mentioned something to me – I told him you had the right to answer for yourself, as a human being, as someone in a committed relationship, as the owner of a pet, first. Do that for me – don't be a copper, just for a minute." I told him what Mark Roscoe had told me in the car. Tony listened. Feroc watched him listening.
I finished speaking – and waited.

"I'll do it."

"Tony -" Feroc reached for him, yelping as some piece of medical equipment reminded him he probably shouldn't be doing that just yet. Tony took hold of his lover's hand, and turned to him.

"I'll be safer undercover, probably, than I am on the streets. I've done UC work before – I know the ropes, and I know how to stay out of trouble. CID'll sort out a convincing legend for me, and I won't have the uniform to draw peoples' attention, and hostility."

"But what about us? How will I know what's going on?"

Tony looked up. "I want Sergeant Gardiner to be one of my handlers, Guv. Feroc's not experienced enough, but she is, and I know she'll keep him in the loop."

"Consider it done."

"Thanks, Guv." A worried frown crossed his face. "Guv – who's been looking after Idaho?"

"That bloody parrot the con Lassiter landed on you? My wife insisted I go and get him. Your keys were in your locker. I put them back there."

"He's at yours?"

"You seem amused, Raglan."

"I just don't see you as a bird man, Guv."

I scowled at him. "I'm not. And I regret ever telling that woman about you and Feroc ending up with the bloody thing. And you know what? My daughter has fallen in love, and wants a bird of her own. I, Anthony, am going to be overrun with things that can't control their own crap."

Tony Raglan was fighting hard not to laugh. "It's one bird, Guv."

"Oh, really? Does it demand some "Idaho show", and scream because you have no bloody idea what show it's on about when it's at yours?"

"He wants *The Big Bang Theory*, Guv. It's on Channel 4, or if its not on telly when he wants it, it'll be online on the on-demand service."

"Oh, right, so I'm just an unpaid valet to a telly-addict, geek-loving parrot, now, am I?"

"He's not that much work, once you get to know him. Out of interest, how did you get his cage to yours? We walked it back from Steve's – he only lives – lived -" there was a flash of something unreadable in Tony's eyes, just for the briefest of moments - "a couple of streets away from mine. You're clear the other side of town, out in the suburbs."

"I know. I had to ask one of the van drivers to come by and load him up for me. Which, incidentally, I will never live down. And he ate my fern. Within an *hour* of being in the bloody house."

"You shouldn't've let him out straight away, Guv."

"I didn't – my wife thought he "might like to feel he was in the jungle", and put his cage near my fern. I've kept that fern alive for over five years, Raglan."

Tony gave up trying not to laugh. It was probably just as well for him that the nurse popped her head round the door just then, to let me know my five minutes were up.

"Get well soon, Raglan – I mean it."

"Well, you know how these things can take time, Guv..."

"Not unless you want to hear what roast parrot tastes like." I stepped out into the corridor. Mark Roscoe got to his feet, and handed me a polystyrene cup of coffee that was more luke than warm. I drank it in a couple of scowling gulps, tossed the cup, and turned to walk away.

"He'll do it. I'm not happy about that. "

"I spoke to the doctor here. He might not be fit, anyway."

I rounded on him. "What? Why? What did he say?"

"There's a possibility he may need a hip replacement. It's not certain, yet, which is why they haven't told him, but, if he does..."

"He'll be medically retired," I finished, my heart sinking at the thought. Tony Raglan was not the kind of copper you could imagine slinking off into what he would see as a dishonourable discharge. He was the kind of copper you saw raising hell as he celebrated thirty years' service, the kind of copper you could see becoming the kind of old man who would raise the same level of hell when he made it into treble figures.

"It's not set in stone, Bill. They want to keep him in for a week, do some more x-rays over that time, and see if things start to resolve themselves. It could just be because of the swelling associated with trauma."

"Or I could be facing having to explain to one of the best coppers I've known why he can't do his job any more. Can you even imagine Tony Raglan signing on at the dole office, for crying out loud?"

Mark Roscoe grinned. "The job coaches, or whatever they call them, would definitely earn their money, that's for damn sure. But it's not going to come to that. Even if Feroc -"

"Oh, god, no. What's wrong with Feroc? Not both of them, Mark – I can't lose both of them."

"It's not as bad as they thought, Bill – they thought he'd fractured his pelvis, but he hadn't – it was some kind of damage that could

be easily repaired with surgery. He'll need a fair amount of physio,
but he'll be fine, given time and rest and a bit of common sense."
My laughter was more relief than anything. "Common sense?
They do know he lives with Tony Raglan, don't they?"
"I think Tony made that quite clear, the  way he was carrying on
before they moved Feroc in with him."
We walked out, laughter fighting fear.

 When I got home, the parrot flew at my face, screaming.
"What the hell is the bird doing loose?!" I shouted, once Idaho
had been sufficiently distracted by a desire to climb the curtains.
Caitlyn came through, whistling and holding something brightly
coloured and child-safe in one hand. "He was sad. He kept crying
– properly crying. He wouldn't eat his dinner. Not even when I put
fresh fruit in, like it says you're supposed to. He was shouting for
Steve – I'm assuming that was his first owner, the man who went
to prison?" I nodded. "And then he was just making
these...choking sounds. I thought he was dying. So I let him out."
She smiled as the parrot landed on my favourite armchair,
marking conquered territory in the time-honoured way. "He
cheered right up, didn't you, sweetie?"
An ancient, reptilian eye rolled inquisitively and challengingly
towards her. "Idaho show. Idaho. Idaho. Idaho show." It sounded
vaguely threatening.
"Apparently he likes *The Big Bang Theory,* Although Raglan's
probably introduced him to Jeremy Clarkson by now."
Caitlyn brightened. "Oh, good! I was worrying about how we
were going to find out what show he meant!" She went over to the
computer in the corner of the room, and began clicking with a
speed I could only envy.  At the first sound of the theme song, the
bird hurled himself across the room, landing on the back of the
computer chair and commencing a frenzied dance. "Idaho!
Idaho!!! Penny!!! Penny! Leonard! Idaho!"
Well, at least making the world right for one person was easy
enough, even if that person were basically a residual dinosaur with
the mentality of a toddler.

### DI Mark Roscoe

"You look shattered, Bill," I greeted my uniformed colleague as he came in for the start of his late shift, just as I was heading down to the canteen for a quick bite.

"Bloody parrots. You know they're basically dinosaurs that refused to die, yes?"

I grinned. "Ah, yes – how *is* Idaho?"

"Bloody demanding. Right now, I'm not sure who's worse – Tony Raglan, or his bloody bird."

"Oh, definitely Raglan – you can cage the parrot."

"As soon as I find one big enough, I'm caging Tony Raglan. He needs to be kept out of harm's way for as long as possible."

"I think they call that false imprisonment, Bill."

"So?"

"So, it's...somewhat frowned upon."

"Only if someone finds out."

I grinned. "You didn't hear the racket Raglan was making when he came round yesterday, before they moved Feroc in with him – people would find out."

"Not if I put Feroc in there with him."

I chuckled. "I wonder if gays are like pandas – they won't mate in captivity."

"Mark! That's out of order!" Bill Wyckham sounded genuinely outraged, Maybe I had crossed a line. I opened my mouth to apologise, but Wyckham kept talking.

"I mean, seriously – Tony Raglan agreeing to a bamboo diet?"

We both had to lean against the wall for support, the laughter that came over us was that strong. It felt good to laugh – it had been far too long.

"Oh, before you go, Bill – tell Tony Raglan, when he's fit, we've got a few old bangers we could use the insurance on. He seems rather good at writing off cars."

Bill Wyckham pulled a face. "Tell me about it. I've got to go and have my ear chewed over the latest one." He sighed. "I think the worst of it is knowing he doesn't mean to do it – that he only means the best, and things just...keep going wrong. It's like he's permanently jinxed, or something."

I nodded. "Yeah. I was reading something about that the other day, on some blog somewhere – apparently, there are people who're literally born to have bad luck, to be victims. It's nothing they've done, or not done, and they can't change it – it just is, like some people are born to be tall, or have ginger hair." I reflected on what I'd just said, and on all the years I'd been a police officer. "It makes sense, when you think about it – I mean, there's some people, we just keep getting called out because something's happened to them. I'm not talking about the domestic violence cases, either."

Bill Wyckham nodded. "I know what you mean. And there probably is something in it, the idea of a born victim, You reckon that's what Tony Raglan is?"

I thought about it, and shook my head. "He's not a victim – he's a catalyst. It's not so much that things happen *to* him as they happen *around* him."

"That makes sense. Anyway, nice chatting, but I'd better get on – the uniform won't put itself on, the Super won't yell at empty air, the troops won't assign their own duties, etc, etc."

I grinned. "Have a good one, Bill."

"You too, Mark – what's left of it."

We parted ways, and I watched him walk away. He looked older, more tired,, as though he were carrying the weight of the world on his shoulders.

I understood. If something like this happened to one of my team, I'd be feeling the same way. It tears you up inside, being responsible for people whom you have to treat as mentally competent adults. You're supposed to protect them, but the very nature of the job they've chosen to do means you *can't* protect them.

If they weren't coppers, they'd be sectioned for their own safety.

My phone rang, just as I reached the canteen – typical.

"Roscoe." I paused, listening. "Right – can you bring him into the canteen? Nice one. See you in a bit." I put the phone back into my pocket, and turned to the weary-but-smiling server, "A cup of coffee and a bowl of cereal ta."

"You expecting company? Only, if you are, I'll leave off closing up for a bit."

"Cheers.."

I turned at the sound of footsteps. A young DC was leading in a tall, well-tailored Indian-looking man. I thought I'd seen him, albeit in a white coat, at St. Ralph's.

"Doctor Parvan, Guv."

The man held out his hand. "Sanjay, please."

"DI Roscoe. Can I get you anything?"

"No, thank you."

The woman behind the counter smiled, and began the process of closing up. I led Sanjay Parvan over to a table, and sat down, pouring out my cardboard carton of cereal, splashing on milk, and turning the whole lot over.

"So – what can I do for you, Doctor?"

"The elderly lady who was involved in the car accident with your police car – she was better today, more lucid, and she talked to one of the nurses. Who phoned me at home, when she came off of her shift, and asked me what she should do about what Mrs. Pearce had said."

"And what had Mrs. Pearce said?"

"Bear in mind, Detective Inspector, that Mrs. Pearce has been through an awful lot, and is eighty-three years of age." I smiled to myself – in less than forty years, Tony Raglan would be eighty-three. Somehow, I couldn't see him taking kindly to people being asked to be more considerate of him "because he's an old boy, bless him."

"She was also capable of driving a car at a hundred miles an hour, doctor. Because, apparently, she saw the devil."

"But that's just it, Detective Inspector – now she is calmer, more lucid, she is certain she saw the murderer. And that that murderer was a woman. A relatively young woman = perhaps in her thirties. She gave a very good description. It did not sound, to me, as though she was delusional, assuming the nurse reported things accurately."

My blood froze. A man with long hair as a murderer, or someone somehow involved with the murder, I could deal with. But I wouldn't even know where to start with a female killer. I don't think I'd ever come across one, certainly not one who acted alone. Women kill in ways that don't draw attention, that look like accidents, or they kill from self-defence.

I sighed. "Can I speak to her? Before she goes home?"

"I think that would be best. I start my rounds at ten tomorrow morning. I will arrange to see her first, if you;d like to be there to question her?"

"Thank you. And thank you for bringing this to my attention, doctor."

"To take a human life, for whatever reason, is not natural. This person needs to be caught, and soon."

"You think they – she? - might kill again?"

"I am not a psychologist, but murder can easily become a habit, I believe."

He stood up, holding out his hand. "Until tomorrow, Inspector'."

I took his hand, and shook it for a second time. "Until tomorrow."

Tomorrow, when I would find out what my prey looked like, according to an eighty-three year old who'd been the other side of the road at the time, and had subsequently been involved in a traumatic accident.

I watched Sanjay Parvan walk away, and had a feeling he'd just caused me more problems than he'd helped solve.

# RAGNAROK

"Well, Andrew Jackson, thirty-one, owner-occupier, unmarried, investment analyst, soon to be late of this parish, I do believe it is time for a meeting, don't you?"

I was watching Andrew Jackson from just a few feet away – it was a weekday, and yet he was at the beach, revelling, it seemed, in a stolen sunny day.

If I hadn't already decided to kill him, that would have made up my mind, the arrogant assumption that, because his salary would be paid come what may, it didn't matter if he didn't show up, if he didn't give a hundred percent.

I can't stand laziness. I work hard at my job – other people should work hard at theirs. After all, they get paid: I don't. At least, not in money.

Jackson was tall, lean, with that sculpted look that only came from spending time at the gym, rather than on genuine self-improvement, or the betterment of society. He was wearing snugly fitting Chino shorts, and a loose, button-down, short-sleeved shirt. His feet were bare, but I didn't doubt for a moment that the leather satchel he'd flung casually onto the sand beside him held a pair of brand-name loafers.

His dark hair was elegantly tousled – the kind of hair style that quietly informed you that its wearer had spend quite a considerable sum of money, and a not insignificant amount of time, to look as though they were an impoverished student who'd just rolled out of bed.

I hated him. If I'd been less restrained, less professional, I would have killed him where he sprawled, simply because he offended my sense of aesthetics.

But I *was* a professional, and a damn good one – I had no intention of throwing that away on a no-account wastrel like Andrew Jackson.

I adjusted my sunglasses, settled back, and picked up my magazine. It was important that Jackson didn't have any reason to pay close attention to me – I would be seeing him later, in about two weeks' time, and I didn't want him noticing me before I was ready,

No chance of that =from the way he pricked up his ears and began to pay attention, in more ways than one, when a group of teenagers, clearly playing hooky from school, began to bounce around with a volleyball a few feet away, he clearly liked his women a lot younger than me.

I knew he did – I'd seen his hard drive. His browse history. The magazines under his bed. That had been very early on in our dalliance, and had confirmed my attraction, my belief that he was the one. Or, at least, the *next* one.

He had made it intolerable that I should allow him to live, had drawn the spirit of righteous rage that informed all of my killings to its full and furious height. Her fire still burned strong, and I whispered to her to be patient.

Not long, now. Two weeks, and Andrew Jackson and I would have our first, and last, date.

## Inspector Bill Wyckham
## LB 81

I sat opposite Mark Roscoe, my head in my hands. "So, let me get this straight – the woman who initially thought she saw a sex-changed Lucifer is now saying that she definitely saw the murderer, and it was definitely a human woman?"

"According to the nurse who related it to the doctor, yes."

"Right, so, at this precise moment in the madness that passes for my life, all we have is third-hand information?"

"Yes, but I'm going out there, to St. Ralph's, to do a formal interview with her tomorrow. Get a more precise description."

I looked up. "A more precise description?! From an old biddy who was across the other side of the road, in a car, focusing on her grandson getting into his house alright, in the very early hours of the morning?! Jesus, Mark – how accurate do you think that description is going to be? We're going to end up with a description that could be almost anyone! The switchboard is going to be flooded with calls saying its someone's brother's ex-girlfriend, or some woman's long-lost daughter, or a Mammy who went off the deep end fifteen years ago, and always prided herself on her long locks..."

"Bill." Mark spoke quietly, too quietly. I couldn't ignore him, and I couldn't talk over him. I settled for scowling at him. "I know who you're thinking of – a woman, someone killed in the vicinity of a house that has known connections to the sex industry – but you can't protect her any more. She gave up the Job the first time she killed. She's just Joe Public, now."

"She's ill, Mark. We did that to her. We destroyed a good officer, a good woman. Tony Raglan knew it would happen – Morgana wasn't the only one who was out of her mind, afterwards. You didn't see Tony, those first few weeks after she was gone."

"No, I didn't. I wasn't posted here, then. But everyone knew about Morgana Cassidy – it's why I was so thorough with Billy Cassidy's background – I couldn't risk him being any kind of connection to her."

I was out of my chair, fists flying across the desk. "Guilt by association?! You bastard, Roscoe!"

He didn't fight me off. Didn't try. Didn't even raise his hands to keep my fists at bay. He just stood there, taking it, waiting until my moment of fury passed.

What a pro. Lothing was lucky to have a man like Mark Roscoe on board, especially at rank level.

I sat back down, slowly, feeling embarrassed and ashamed. I'd behaved like a daft kid, for no reason. "Sorry, Mark. Don't know what came over me." I fidgeted with my shirt collar, and stared out of the window.

"It's alright." Roscoe straightened his own shirt. "I could have phrased that better, probably. Anyway, as you said, I wasn't here, after it happened. Tell me about Tony Raglan."

"He was spoiling for a fight – going for anyone, whether they'd asked for it or not. I had to drag him off a prisoner, more than once – we hushed things up, calmed everyone down, but it was close, too damn close. He was told to take some leave, come back in a couple of weeks or so."

"He didn't?"

"Oh, no – he did. He completely vanished. Off the radar entirely. No one knew where he was. Then, three weeks later, he turns up in a right state."

"How d'you mean?"

"He had to have lost at least a couple of stone. In three weeks. His clothes were hanging off him – I'm not exaggerating. He looked ill, properly ill. Exhausted. That first week back, he didn't even want to go out in Lima-Bravo One - he volunteered for every station duty going. And no one saw him eat, not once, in a week.

"That doesn't sound right."

"It wasn't right. He never even finished a whole cup of coffee – not when he was here, not from what people saw, anyway. He'd take a couple of gulps, then leave it. He was lost, Mark. Something had broken in him, too, the same way it had with Morgana."

There was silence between us for a moment, before Mark Roscoe

83

spoke. "Is it possible there was something...that they were... I mean, I know Tony's gay, but a lot of people, older people, they don't always just admit it, the way kids do, do they?"

I shook my head. "A lot of people assumed there was something – no one knew Tony was gay, not then. We barely knew anything about him, really, for all he'd become part of the furniture. Maybe there was. Maybe one or other of them simply wished there was. Maybe they'd tried it, and it hadn't worked out. No one knew anything for certain except that Morgana was crazy, and Tony was as good as. And then the murders started. And, strangely, that seemed to bring Tony round. Andrew, the Inspector at the time, suggested that when Tony was on leave, he'd gone looking for Morgana, and the way he'd been when he came back was down to not being able to find her. He thought that the murders, with her call sign at the scene, caused Tony to rally because he knew, even if he didn't know where Morgana was, that she was alright. If she was killing, she was alive. And functional enough that she could execute a murder without getting caught."

Roscoe nodded. "That takes some doing, definitely." He paused, and looked at me, something terrifyingly serious coming into his eyes. "Bill, I need you to be honest with me on this – no protecting your boy, here: if Raglan had found Morgana, if he knew she was back in Lothing – would he tell you? Would he tell us?"

The Royal "Us" - "Us" meaning the Force. Meaning any copper, anywhere. Us meaning: Would Tony Raglan, stalwart of the service, do the right thing if it meant a one-time friend and colleague ended up in handcuffs, ended up in prison, a life sentence of bars and loneliness? I knew what Mark Roscoe was asking – but I didn't know the answer.

I shook my head. "I want to say yes, of course he would. I want to be furious that you even needed to ask that question. I want to trust him. But..."

"But?"

I sighed. "But the truth, the honest answer, is: I don't know. Tony Raglan is good at keeping secrets, and I think he's the dangerous kind of person, who *enjoys* keeping secrets. It's possible that he wouldn't tun her in, if he'd found her. If she'd come home. It would be right according to his lights – he...he sees things differently to other people, sometimes."

"I'd noticed." Mark picked up a pen, twiddling it between thumb and forefinger. "But he did tell people about Feroc, in the end."

I shook my head. "No. *Feroc* told people – or, rather, Feroc made it obvious. Tony just confirmed it, and decided to live in the light of that particular revelation." I decided to try and change tack. "What do we know about Claire Jakely?"

Roscoe shook his head. "Not much, not yet – my team are doing the preliminaries now. So far, so normal. No criminal record, one record of contact with the police – uniformed officers were called after a neighbour apparently made threats. No further action – it was one of those they-said-she-said deals. No hope of working out the truth of it. We'll send someone round to speak to the neighbour concerned, assuming it's the same person – Claire Jakely certainly hadn't moved in the intervening three years, anyway."

"Three years is a long time to go between threatening someone and killing them."

"Unless there were other incidents, afterwards, that Claire didn't report because she didn't believe we gave a toss."

That, sadly, was more than likely. While people understood that we simply didn't have the resources to sort out every single incident, to punish every transgression against them, they tended, if they felt they'd been brushed off once, not to bother us again. That was more of a problem for marginalised groups, though – the middle classes, of which Claire Jakely had most definitely been a member, tended to go for annoyed, rather than resigned, when they felt they weren't being listened to.

"I'll see if we've got anything on file – even if she didn't make a complaint herself, someone else might have done. Neighbours like that don't tend to just make life a misery for one person." I remembered an altercation I'd picked up back when I'd been a Sergeant – I'd recognised the address as being somewhere near Tony Raglan's place, and had turned up to find him calmly and concisely schooling his then next-door-neighbour, who'd later moved, in what was and was not well-mannered behaviour. I pulled the car up a distance away, and myself and my constable sat and watched – the crowd gathered round seemed pleased that something was finally being done, and this wasn't the first time we'd had reports of anti-social behaviour from this particularly woman and her single-mother teenage kid. Everything from spitting at people to threatening to poison their dogs, through noise complaints and rumours of drug use.

When we finally and casually strolled up, the woman was backed against a brick wall, her daughter screaming obscenities from inside the house, as her mother yelled at her to "Shurrup! For god's sake, just shurrup you stupid cow!" and the teenage mum's young child screamed.

Tony stood, hands in his pockets, anger on his face. I 'd glanced at the woman by the wall. "You hurt?" She'd shaken her head.

"He never laid a finger on 'er – if 'er or that bitch brat of 'ers says otherwise, they're lying cows, the pair of 'em!" a tired-looking middle-aged woman, eyes bright with battle light, had helpfully informed us.

"So, what did happen here?" I'd asked.

"That cow come out, starting on my boy when he was minding his own business, walking the dog – she threatened to drive her car into them both! Said the dog'd gone for her cat – bloody nonsense, Byron doesn't bother about cats. Then she called my boy a faggot, just because he'd told her daughter she was a manky slag. Which she is – you don't see a father for that brat of hers, do you? Just like she ain't got one. And off down the shop for vodka at all hours, usually in her bloody pyjamas! It's a disgrace. And neither of 'em lift a finger to do an honest day's work – god knows how they're getting away with that! Anyway, he comes home, sees her laying in to my Robbie, and gives her what-for."

"About time someone did. Woman never used to behave like that. No one did, not in my day", added an elderly man who was standing by the safety of his open front door.

I'd looked at my officer, his eyes brightly innocent, his posture relaxed, no blood on his hands or his shirt. "Tony?"

"She needed to be taught a lesson. I taught it. No blood, no foul."

I'd turned to the woman. "Do you want to make a complaint?"

She'd shaken her head, furiously. "Right. Get up, get indoors. Look to your daughter and granddaughter. And don't you dare let me hear of you making threats to kill peoples' pets, or shouting abuse at other people in this street – we've been called about that more than once, not to mention the screaming that goes on in your house. I know social services have had contact with you and your daughter – I'm guessing you don't want to have to speak to them again, do you?"

She'd shaken her head, getting slowly to her feet, her eyes never leaving Tony's face, the wary watchfulness of an animal that knows it's met a bigger, stronger beast.

"Right. Well, try and behave like civilised human beings, rather than howler monkeys." I'd watched her scuttle inside, seen the window slam closed, heard the door being hurriedly locked. I'd turned to the crowd, many of whom were already drifting back to their houses. Excelsior Street wasn't the kind of place people tended to loiter once uniforms appeared.

"Tony – get inside, and don't let me be called out to anything involving you again."

He'd given me that lazy, infuriating grin he was so good at, and loped back to his front door. "Tony."

"Sarge?" He'd turned, key in the lock.

"Why don't you move somewhere a bit more upmarket? You could easily afford it. Half the people here are on the dole, a quarter of the rest are running one scam or another, and the remainder are either retired or run down from minimum-wage drudgery. Why do you want to live here?"

He'd thought for a moment, then smiled, a little sadly, I'd thought. "Because people don't ask questions here."

I hadn't known what he'd meant by that until two years ago. Until the shooting in the Heart of Darkness. Until Feroc, and all the revelations that came out at that time.

Mark Roscoe nodded. "Good idea. We're having a bit of difficulty tracing her next of kin. You couldn't send a couple of uniform round to her place in the morning, could you, give it a spin for us?"

"Sure. Do we have anything on them?"

He shook his head. "She didn't record a next of kin with her GP, and she appears to have been self-employed, or at least that's what she told the tax man."

"Doing what?"

"Lifestyle consultancy, whatever that is when it's at home. Sounds like a tax dodge to me – living the high life on a credit card, then writing it all off as 'legitimate business expenses.' Nice work if you can get it."

I laughed. "Don't let Tony Raglan in on that – I can see him thinking it's a great idea for his retirement occupation. Only, in his case, the focus will be on fast cars, high-end casinos, and gin palaces."

"Does he gamble, then?"

I grinned. "Yes, but it's alright, because he wins. And if he stops winning, he stops playing."

"How the hell do you know this?"

"My missus and I went to that new casino at Yarmouth when it opened, just for a look-see. He was there already. I kept out of his way, and just watched him. He knew what he was doing, no question. And a couple of the other pros there – gamblers, not the other kind – clearly knew him. And the casino let him run a tab – they don't do that unless you've got references from at least two other establishments."

Roscoe whistled. "Well well. You learn something new every day."

"Indeed. I think he uses his casino winnings to further his interest in art."

"He's interested in *art*? Are we actually talking about the same Tony Rag – well, ignore that: he did date that painter bloke who was caught up in the scam Eastern Rise were running, apparently. He kept *that* quiet."

I shook my head. "That's what I mean, about him being good at keeping secrets – he knows how to do it. Because he *didn't* keep it quiet, not in the conventional sense. We all knew he was seeing someone called Max, we just didn't realise Max was in possession of a Y chromosome and an Adam's apple. That's a professional's way of keeping a secret – to let everyone think you're *not* keeping a secret. To appear completely open, without giving anything away."

 Mark Roscoe stood up, stretching languidly, like a contented cat, only with a little more claw. "You're right, Bill. Keep an eye on Raglan – he's a dark horse, and, like you say, they can be dangerous." He glanced at his watch. "Anyway, I'd better get on. See you later."

"Later."

I sat in silence, long after the echo of the door closing had faded, and reflected on the fact that Tony Raglan had been very good at giving me the impression that I knew him very well, when, just like everyone else, except perhaps from Max and Feroc, and possibly Morgana, I hadn't known him at all.

## Sonia

I could hear the laughter from halfway down the corridor. I burst into the room, a scowl of mock outrage making my face darker than it usually was. I hoped I looked like a coming storm – that was my aim, anyway.

"You two! This is a *hospital!* There are sick people in here! And you yapping on fit to wake the dead!"

Tony Raglan smiled – that lazy, sexy smile that made every straight woman wonder how he could possibly be gay, every lesbian wonder why she was, and every gay man wonder what his chances were. I bet it annoyed the hell out of straight men, who'd never been much good at managing their natural, human curiosity about other men. "Sorry, nurse. We didn't realise we were being so loud." He tugged at his earlobe. "Maybe the accident affected our hearing, or something."

"Or maybe neither of you were spanked and told to hush nearly enough when you were naughty, obnoxious, loud little boys." I smiled, trying and failing to imagine Tony Raglan in shorts and a stripey t-shirt, sailing brightly coloured wooden boats on park ponds, climbing trees, ordering gobstoppers. Feroc, with his tousled mane of dirty blond hair, I could readily picture as a child. He would have been the kind of boy who got mistaken for a girl until he was about seven or eight, and who broke hearts from that day forward. I probably wasn't the first person to wonder what had drawn him to Tony Raglan.

Tony Raglan, who was grinning broadly. "You can spank me any time you like, Sonia.."

"I didn't think you played that way."

"I don't, but as we always tell the hetros, don't knock it 'til you"ve tried it."

"Yeah, well, I don't like it rough – giving *or* receiving, thank you. Now – hold out your arms, both of you – I need to check your temperature. You first, Tony – the doctor was concerned you were running a fever, which would potentially mean you'd been inconsiderate enough to pick up an infection. As though the NHS isn't spending enough money on you."

"You should be looking forward to privatisation, then – you'll make a fortune off of me."

"More like we'll *spend* a fortune chasing your unpaid bills, while you smile at the girls in the accounts department and spin plausible lies."

Tony Raglan looked up, an expression of seemingly genuine outraged hurt in his eyes. When he spoke, his voice was viciously quiet. "I always pay my bills. Always. And I always pay them with my own money." Feroc glanced over, worried, and reached for Tony's hand. I was shocked when Tony shook his head, just once, his eyes still focused, furiously, on me.

"Alright – I'm sorry. I didn't mean to offend you. Anyway, privatisation won't happen, not if the unions and the people have anything to say about it."

"That's what you think."

"Look, I'm not blind – I know there's been hospitals sold off. I know people are losing their jobs. But people are fighting it. People -"

"People don't have a clue. I've been around the people they're *really* fighting, Sonia – not the disposable puppets that make the papers or get in front of the cameras. The real enemies? They"re bloody terrifying, when you sit beside them. They know what they want, and they won't stop until they get it. And they don't care what they have to do in the process."

I licked my lips, watching his face for any sign that he was on a wind up. I didn't find one.

"Well, can't you – the police, I mean – stop them? If they're breaking the law?"

He barked out a laugh. "Why do you think our budgets and numbers get cut, year on year? There's not enough of us to stop them, even if the Courts weren't rigged in their favour."

"How do you know this? You say you've met these people – where?"

"Casinos."

Feroc looked at Tony, a puzzled frown crossing his face. "But you don't – Oh."

"Where did you think I got the money from? Art doesn't exactly consider coppers' salaries in its pricing, does it?"

"I...I thought.... Tony, you're not ..."

"No. I'm good at what I do, Feroc. At *everything* I do. If I'm not good at it, I don't do it."

I looked between the two of them, finally focusing on Tony.

"You're not talking about a couple of hours at a charity gala, are you?"

"No. I'm talking about a couple of hours a night. Almost every night. Mostly online, but I try and get to an actual casino at least once a month. It's been a while, what with one thing and another, though."

Feroc stared at him. "I use my savings to buy art. I assumed you were doing the same sort of thing."

"You assumed correctly. My savings just come from a different source than yours, that's all."

"If you were in debt..."

"You'd be the last to know. I take care of my own, and that means never telling them things that might cause them to worry unnecessarily. If I were in debt, I'd sort it."

I wanted to say something about how caring for someone meant not lying to them, how it meant telling them first when something was wrong, but somehow the words came out wrong.

"Let's get your temperature taken, shall we?"

Tony nodded. "Yeah. It's getting a little hot in here."

"You should be used to the heat." Feroc's voice was bitter. Tony looked stunned. "Fer – what's wrong? We're not in any kind of trouble, we're not struggling. I'm good at gambling, Fer. I know what I'm doing."

"Yeah? That's what everyone thinks, until it's too late."

"Fer, trust me, I stop well before that point."

"Until the day you don't see that you're coming up to that point." Feroc Hanson turned his face away from his lover. "I never trust anyone who says 'trust me.' It's a rule that's served me very well so far."

I paused, the thermometer in mid-air. This really wasn't the right time.

"Feroc." It was a pleading, a whispered whine. "Feroc, please – look, if you have a problem with the idea of me gambling, then I won't. No questions. I'll stop, straight away. I don't have a problem with that."

"And then I get to be the arsehole who stopped you having fun? No thanks."

"Dammit, Feroc." Tony was growling, and I saw physical pain flare in his eyes. "Dammit, I'm in fucking agony here, and you're trying to walk out on me. I don't *care* about gambling, Feroc – I do it because it's there,  because I'm good at it, and yes, because I enjoy it. But I'll find other things to enjoy. I *care* about you."

There was silence – too much silence. Then, slowly, Feroc turned to look at Tony, and, slowly, he held out his hand again.

This time, Tony took it.

"I'm sorry, Tone."

"So am I. I should have told you – I didn't realise you had such a problem with it."

"Why didn't you tell me? If it wasn't that you thought I'd have a problem with it, why didn't you tell me?"

Tony shook his head, wincing in pain. "I don't know. I suppose part of me just enjoys keeping secrets, somehow."

Feroc studied him. "Yeah. I thought we'd talked about that."

"We had. I guess... I suppose keeping secrets is my addiction, if I have one."

Feroc gave a weak smile. "And isn't it typical? They don't have a twelve-step programme for that."

We all laughed, the kind of laughter that spoke of danger passed, for the moment. I waved the thermometer. "Can I *please* take your temperature now? Y'know – get on with my *job?*"

Feroc's temperature was fine – high, but lower than it had been at last check. He'd had quite a time of it in surgery, so I wasn't surprised.

I frowned at Tony. "I'm not happy about this. Your temperature's been rising every check from the time you came in. How are you feeling?"

"Fine. Not cold, not hot – it hurts, it hurts like hell, all over, but I'm fine otherwise."

"Any stomach cramps, headaches, nausea?"

"I don't think so."

"Hm." I frowned at the thermometer. "I'm going to get the doctor in. You might need a course of antibiotics. You're not allergic to anything, are you?"

"Not that I'm aware of."

"Have you been prescribed antibiotics before?"

"I was prescribed a whole load of stuff, when I got out after I was shot. I think there was morphine in there – that was good stuff. I can see why people get addicted to that."

"Well, antibiotics would have been in the mix. If you had no problems, it's fairly safe to say you're not allergic to them."

"So, when can we go home?"

"That depends on how you respond to the antibiotics. But, if you need to be kept in once Feroc's been cleared for discharge, I'll arrange for him to stay on – it saves the tax payer money paying for visiting carers, if you go home together and help each other through. It should only be a couple of days more, at most."

Feroc swallowed, hard. "I'll be alright, if you do need to discharge me sooner – I know how stretched things are for you guys. I can get my sister to come over and help out. She's okay with stuff."

Tony looked anxious, then sighed. "Yeah. And I don't know how Idaho's coping. He was just starting to settle with us – the sooner he's back home, with people he knows, the better."

I smiled. "Yeah. I think your Inspector feels much the same."

Tony laughed. "Idaho giving him grief, is he?"

"Oh, no more than you do, probably – he just can't put you in a cage when he's had enough of you.  Now – I'm going to see if I can find a doctor anywhere around the place. You two – *behave!*"

The laughter started half a second after I'd stepped away from the door.  I smiled. Those boys were going to be alright.

## Edna

I know I shouldn't have panicked like that, that it was dangerous, and very silly, to drive off so fast. Fred was very annoyed with me – especially about the car, I think, but about everything, really. He told me I'd been daft, that I'd just seen someone, and let my mind play tricks on me. He reckoned I'd probably heard about the goings-on in that house on the news at some point, and, seeing someone outside, in the dark, I'd been silly and panicked when I shouldn't have.

But the thing is, I've always been very good at reading energy. I don't tell people about it – and certainly not Fred: he doesn't approve of any of that sort of thing. I can't even take him to fetes and things if there's likely to be a tarot reader or some such there – he'll go over and start having a real go at them. The last time, it was some poor young girl, she only looked about twenty or so, and so thin, with terribly pale skin. He frightened her, I think. Then her husband or boyfriend or whatever arrived, and gave Fred what for. I was glad she had someone looking out for her.

I *can* read energy, though, and what I'd felt that night, looking at that woman – it was definitely a woman, I was sure of that, even though Fred had tried to tell me it was probably a man with long hair, that women didn't go in for killing, not like that, anyway, that I'd been watching too much *Miss Marple* – was a definite sense of wrongness. Of evil. Her energy had been black, like a coiling snake, and it had felt cold and scaly and reptilian. She'd killed someone, or was about to kill someone – I could tell. And I'd panicked, and that panic had led to … well, to everything else.

I did hope those two police officers were alright. I remembered how worried the young one had seemed. It must have been his Dad with him – it was nice when boys followed their fathers into jobs, especially jobs like that. I hoped they were both alright – I don't know how I'd live with myself, if a father had to live on without his son, or if the poor boy had to bury his father while he was still injured himself. I wondered if his mother had been told, how she was managing without her husband to help her. I couldn't think what I'd do if I ever lost Fred, although I knew it would come, and probably fairly soon – he was five years older than me, after all. I'd been a mere chit of a girl, barely twenty-one, when we'd met, and him all grown-up and sophisticated, seeming far older than he was. He'd been a gentleman, always – the rakishness was an affectation, to charm the dolly-birds, as he called us girls. But he'd never gone after anyone else once we were settled together as a couple. He'd always been good to me.

I was so cross with Sandra, though – it wasn't right, a woman working all night like she did. Mind you, it was that good-for-nothing Eric was more to blame. If he hadn't been the wastrel he was, if he hadn't left at the first opportunity, my Sandra wouldn't have had to go to work, and she'd've been bringing Tom home.

Suddenly, I felt terribly cold – if *she'd* been bringing Tom home, the murderess might have killed them both, assuming that they'd actually seen her – young people have better eyesight, after all. She might have assumed they'd seen her. Sandra might actually have done so, and in more detail than I had.

It had been good to see Sandra this afternoon. She'd been very kind and reassuring – she and Tom were going to move in with me and Fred – Tom could sleep in the spare room, she'd have the sofa – and look after me until I was properly well. She was a good girl, my Sandra – I just wished she'd never met Eric. Everything would have been alright if he hadn't come along. Although I wouldn't have Tom. Sandra was my only child, and I adored little Tommy. No, I wouldn't wish Eric out of existence, because Eric had given me Tom.

Poor Tom – how was he going to get to work and back, on the nights Sandra had to work, now I didn't have a car? The doctor had said I probably wouldn't be able to drive again – who'd sort Tom out, and look after Fred? And what about when Sandra's car was in the garage? How was she supposed to get to work?

Oh, it was all so worrying, and it was all because of my stupid energy reading – if I were normal, I wouldn't have thought twice about that woman, and none of this would have happened.

## DI Mark Roscoe

"Hello, Edna. Fred. I'm sure you remember me? Detective Inspector Roscoe, Lothing CID." I turned to face the harassed-looking blonde woman who was perched on the end of the hospital bed, allowing the elderly Fred to occupy the single chair in the room. "Sandra?"

She nodded. "Yes. Your uniformed officers came round yesterday, and told me about Mum." She patted her mother's hand, almost abstractedly, yet still not without tenderness. "I feel so guilty – if I hadn't taken that job, if I wasn't working nights, I'd've been the one picking Tom up, and I probably wouldn't even have noticed anything – we wouldn't have been sitting out on the road, for a start."

"I don't see why that lad can't sort himself out and get a car of his own. Useless layabout, just like his father."

"Fred!"

"Well, it's true. He shouldn't be expecting people to fetch and carry him here, there and everywhere. When I was his age, I was cycling ten miles each way to work."

"Dad....we've been through this. Tom has Asperger's. It's not safe for him to cycle into town, not with all the traffic there is these days. It would be alright if everyone cycled, and was sensible, but that's not the case."

"We never had none of this Asperger's nonsense when I was young. All these modern fads – Asperger's this, sex-change that. It's just kids wanting to make a show of themselves, that's all it is."

"Dad, what has Asperger's got to do with people having sex-changes?" Sandra sounded wearily resigned – I got the feeling that Fred was often like this, whether he was anxious about something or not. My father was much the same.

"There was some programme, on the telly, about how there's men making themselves into women, but they all have this Asperger's thing. So it *is* related!" Fred's triumphant glare was the mirror of my own father's. I could hear my mother's tired voice: "Don't upset him, Mark – he doesn't understand what the world's become; it's not how either of us remembers it, y'see, and, well, it worries him..." No use arguing that maybe he'd be less worried by the state of the world if he allowed people to challenge his assumptions on it – my mother was foolishly and faithfully devoted to her husband, as I sensed Edna was to Fred. She patted his arm now, frail and trembling.

"But Tommy's not having a sex-change, is he?"

"He probably will do, once people stop caring about this Asperger's he apparently has. What even is that, anyway?"

"It's a kind of autism, Dad."

"It can't be autism – when kids've got autism, they're screaming and messing themselves, running wild everywhere. Be better to drown the poor buggers at birth."

"Fred!"

"All I'm saying is, if he can manage a job, he can manage learning to drive, or getting his backside on a bicycle."

"Sandra's right, though, Freddy – there's ever so many cars, these days. There weren't when we were young, only a few, and they didn't go so fast, you see."

"What've they got all these computer games for, then, if it's not to teach them how to manage in the world? That's what they say they're for – teaching skills and what not. Wasting time, more like! Layabouts, this generation, expecting everything for nothing."

Sandra finally lost her patience, and got to her feet. "What, like you and your bloody guaranteed pension? Your free prescriptions? Your free bus pass? Your winter-bloody-fuel-allowance that you don't even bloody *use*? Your free TV licence? All the carrying on in the papers, the minute someone suggests you might give some of that up! And don't start on that you 'paid in' for that – you didn't. The government pissed your pension contributions up the wall, and didn't have the balls to tell you. *I'm* paying for your pension – people my age! And your bloody free this, free that, I-lived-through-rationing-so-give-give-give. I won't get my pension until I'm nearly seventy – and it damn well won't be triple-locked and gilt-edged! Tommy probably won't get anything at all. All his generation have ever asked for is the government to pay the cost of them getting a decent education, so they can get a decent job, and be part of society, not get left behind scrabbling about on the minimum wage while the cost of living goes up each year, and everything's cut to the bone because your generation expects and demands and snatches, snatches, snatches, without realising it's all bloody gone – that you've used it all up, because you're so fucking selfish!"

"Sandra! Don't swear at your father!"

But Sandra had stormed off, before, I suspected, the redness around her eyes became tears she didn't want a stranger and an angry man to see. I closed my eyes, wishing I wasn't thinking of all the times before that I'd had to watch women running away from male anger, and been unable to do anything about it, because, legally, "nothing had happened." Nothing had happened, but there was damage done.

"Women. Too emotional, that's their problem. Shouldn't raise boys on their own, they shouldn't – no wonder we've got so many Nancy boys pansying about the place." Fred looked at me. "Bet your lot wish it was still illegal, eh? Proper man's job, being a copper. No place for Nancies in the uniform, eh?"

It was my turn to lose my patience – although I did manage, just, to keep my temper.

"For your information, Mr. Pearce, two of my finest officers, men who go out, every day, never knowing what they might walk into, whether that day might be the day they don't make it home, one of whom was shoot a little less than two years ago, and has been stabbed more times than he can remember, who has gone into burning buildings to rescue people, who nearly drowned going into the sea in the middle of the 2014 surge to rescue a young child who'd been swept off the promenade while her mother was walking her home from her grandparents' house, thinking she could beat the storm because they only lived five minutes along the coast road, are gay men. But you wouldn't know it to look at them, and they're no less ready to go out and give a hundred percent than any of my other officers. They have the complete respect of their colleagues, and the complete confidence of their superiors. Those men, incidentally, and the quick-thinking of one of them, especially, are the sole reason your wife is here now, and well enough to go home tomorrow."

There was a stunned silence. I could feel my anger burning still. I'd never been affected like this before by any of the crap coppers encounter on a daily basis – ignorance, bigotry, outright hatred, violence, the worst kind of sick ravings. I hadn't agreed with it, of course, hadn't wanted to listen to it a minute longer than I had to, but it had never made me so furiously angry that I would have gladly killed someone over it.

And, in a moment of clarity, I understood what the younger generation were talking about, on social media, when they said people needed to be 'woke' – 'woke' was this feeling of passionate rage, the blind, furious certainty that no one would ever be allowed to talk like that about other human beings again. It was a wild feeling, a powerful feeling – a beautiful feeling. It struck me, standing by that hospital bed, that if everyone felt like this, all the time, about all the 'isms' of the world, all the injustice, all the lack of dignity and respect and compassion, then the world would change in a heartbeat.

And it might become the kind of world where my job was a lot easier, the kind of world where coppers like Tony Raglan could sleep soundly at night, the kind of world where the emergency services didn't have a recruitment crisis, a morale crisis, or a funding crisis. The kind of world, perhaps, where we weren't needed, or at least were only needed to be of genuine help, rather than to corral and control, and pick up the pieces.

I took a slow, shaking breath, tasting sulphur. "And no. I wouldn't want homosexuality to be illegal again, just as I wouldn't want Britain to even begin to entertain the idea of not allowing certain people to use certain bathrooms. My job, the job of all police officers everywhere, is made a hundred times harder, public sympathy is torn away from us a hundredfold, when we are commanded and expected to police peoples' private lives. I don't care who someone loves as long as that person is able to consent to what happens within that love, and is not harmed by any expression of it, or by the person who claims to love them." I paused, swallowed, and turned to the old lady in the hospital bed. "Now. You told a nurse, yesterday, that you saw a woman, and you thought she might have killed someone. Can you tell me about that?"

"Oh...oh yes, yes, of course. Those poor officers – I didn't realise – the one in the passenger seat, he seemed so young...but then people with blond hair do look young, often, don't they? Are they alright, those two boys?"

*Boys*. They'd been men, before, even when Edna had thought Feroc was Tony's son, rather than his lover. And now she knew the truth, they were boys, both of them. It was a quieter form of prejudice than her husband's, but it was still there. "If you could focus on what you saw on the night of the accident, please?"

"Oh, yes, of course. Oh, it all seems so very long ago, and yet it wasn't, really, was it? I can see her clearly, the way she lifted her head – like a cat hearing a little bird that it wants to pounce on."

"I don't like cats," Fred muttered, sullenly determined not to be left out. *No*, I thought, *you don't like much, do you?* I wondered if he loved his wife – clearly he must have done once, but did he still? It was part of the reason I'd never got close enough to a woman for the talk to turn to marriage – I was terrified that I'd marry someone I was in love with, and wake up one day to discover the love wasn't there any more. I wondered if Tony or Feroc ever feared that. I wondered if Bill Wyckham feared it, or had experienced it. I'd have to ask him, one day. I could ask him: we were equals, in more than just rank. I couldn't even begin to imagine how I'd put that question to Feroc, and certainly not to Tony Raglan.

I smiled at Edna. "I know what you mean. What else did you notice?"

"Her hair. I think it was blonde – it looked very pale, anyway. If it had been dark, with the shadows and everything, I might not have noticed her. She must have been dressed in all black, because I couldn't make out her body, not really, except she wasn't plump.

Mind you, she wasn't skinny, either. She looked almost like a man, really, although not quite as broad. But I'm certain it was a woman. Her face was quite round. Men don't really have round faces, do they?"

Tony Raglan did, but Edna was right: even his wasn't the soft roundness you got with women. As I'd overheard one of the WPCs joking to her colleagues, Tony Raglan's face looked like a cricket ball that had gone into the crowd and been grabbed by an attending Staffordshire Bull Terrier. That had been before any of us knew about him being gay, and I'd felt a passing sense of sorrow for him, that women would casually talk about him in such disparaging tones. Interestingly, I hadn't heard them do so since his sexuality had become public knowledge. I wondered why that was.

"So, you're as sure as you can be that this was a woman?"

"Yes. She seemed quite tall, although things do look different to how they are, when it's dark, don't they? She might have just been average."

"But she definitely wasn't particularly short?" I was scribbling notes, my own peculiar, and most definitely not 'authorised', in any sense of the word, brand of shorthand cluttering the page. I hoped like hell my notebooks were never requisitioned for an inquiry – no one else would have a hope of interpreting half the things I'd written over the weeks and months and years.

Edna shook her head. "Oh, no. I'd have noticed that – being short myself, I always notice other short people. I'm four feet eleven inches. But I usually wear heels, you see, just small ones, but it means people don't notice so much."

"When you say she was tall, do you mean – forgive me if I put this awkwardly – do you mean that she was tall in comparison to you, or that she would have been tall in comparison to someone of average height?"

"She was at least as tall as Sandra. She's five feet seven."

"Bloody elephant of a woman," Fred muttered from his corner.

Edna, to her credit, glared at him. "Well, if she is, it's your genes made her that way, isn't it? All the women on my side of the

family are short. And don't you start on with your genetic
inferiority nonsense – it didn't bother you when we were courting,
did it, Frederick Pearce?"

I fought to suppress a smile. I didn't need to worry about Edna –
she had the measure of her man, it seemed.

"So, a blonde-haired woman, at least five feet seven, of average
build, on the lean side. Anything else?"

"No, I'm sorry. It was dark, and I wasn't really looking, not
especially."

"That's alright," I smiled, even though it wasn't, really. It was
nothing to go on, a description that would match a hundred
women. "You did well to notice that much."

"Oh, my Edna's very observant. She spots all the mistakes in the
newspapers. They oughta employ her, they do. It doesn't look
good, a newspaper making mistakes. She'd sort them out." Fred
sounded proud of his wife's observational skills, and I reassessed,
yet again, my impression of their relationship. Very possibly Fred
was just a bewildered individual, suddenly aware that his time was
nearly up, and flailing about trying to make some sense of it all.

We'd all been there, and most of us would be there several times
before we reached Frederick Pearce's age. It was a frightening
thing, to be faced with your own irrelevance in the grand scheme
of things.

"What happens now?"

"Well, now you rest, and I think the hospital are going to
discharge you, later. I'll go back to my station, and see if I can find
any people with criminal records for this sort of thing who match
the description you've given me. I've got officers looking for
forensic evidence, too."

"Oooh, like on the telly?"

I nodded. "Exactly like that. If they find enough, it might mean
you don't have to worry about going to Court."

"Oh, I'm not worried about that – what's the worst someone can
do to you, if you say you saw them doing something wrong, and
they get away with it? Come after you and send you to your
Maker?" She giggled. "Well, I'm nearly there, anyway. It makes

no odds to me. If you need me in Court, and I'm still about, I'll be there."

"What're you on about, if you're still about? You'll live forever, you will."

I hadn't heard Sandra come back, but she was suddenly there, standing by the bed, her face looking suspiciously clean. She leaned over, and smoothed back her mother's hair. "I've spoken to the doctor, Mum. He wants to sort you out some prescriptions, then I can take you home. Tom's making spaghetti bolognese."

"Oh, I love spaghetti bolognese! Will he make that cheesy bread he makes to go with it?"

Sandra smiled. "Absolutely. It would never occur to Tom that you could make spaghetti bolognese without cheesy garlic bread." She turned to me, the smile still in place. "He's not incapable. He can cook, he knows about managing money, things like that. And he does really well at work, because it's all about following instructions. He wouldn't manage in an office or a shop, but he does alright at the theatre. His boss is nice – he looks out for him."

I smiled back. "That's good. He sounds  like a lovely lad."

"He is. The absolute best." Sandra glared at her father as she spoke, and, for once, Fred didn't have anything to say.

 I said my goodbyes, promised to pass on Edna's best wishes to Tony and Feroc, and wandered out, through the maze of corridors that pretty much typifies any hospital anywhere, and paused by the lifts. I glanced at my watch.  Yes; plenty of time before I'd be missed, murder inquiry notwithstanding.

## Inspector Bill Wyckham
## LB 81

"Well, it can't be Morgana Cassidy, then. She had curly dark hair."
Mark Roscoe shook his head. "It could still be here, Bill – she
could have had her hair straightened, dyed -"
"Mark, come on! This woman was three stops past Barking.
There's no way she'd be with it enough to sort out her hair. And
besides, the runes aren't her MO. She does tarot cards, with her
old shoulder number on."
"People change their MO. Especially if they're changing their
victims – she's previously gone after sex offenders and human
traffickers, right? Well, it's unlikely Claire Jakely was either –
which implies she's targeting a different group of people, now. For
a different reason."
"Or that it's not Morgana. It's someone else."
"Two female killers, Bill? Come on – you know the odds on that.
And in the same region? It's almost impossible."
"Almost." But, even as I spoke, I knew I was fighting a losing
battle. And I hadn't even told Roscoe about the other thing, yet. I
would have to, though, and he'd become suspicious if he found
out I'd kept it from him. "But you might be right – I don't want
you to be, and part of me still thinks you're not, but..." I sighed. "I
went to the hospital last night, I spoke to Tony. And Feroc, of
course, but more so Tony. I asked him, casually, what his
relationship with Morgana had been like – I phrased it as I'd been
thinking about her, lately, and remembered he'd been the one to
say we should get her out. I spun it that I'd been reminded by your
request for him to go undercover, assuming he's well enough
come the time. I think he bought it, Anyway, turns out Morgana
Cassidy knew he was gay long before Feroc's arrival. She knew
about Max. Seems she had a crush on Tony, and, when he went
out on a welfare check, she...well, she tried to...y'know."
"She tried to get him into bed with her?"
"Yeah. Told him not to worry about Max, that 'she', as we all
assumed Max was, would never find out. That it could be a station

fling – they're fairly common, despite, or perhaps because, they're frowned upon. Apparently she was...quite insistent. So he told her the truth about Max. Called him, had him speak to Morgana."

"How did she take that?"

"Well, apparently. She apologised for being so forward, talked about how lonely and stressed out she was feeling. They stayed friends, until...well, until Morgana left."

"And?"

I glanced up. "Bill, there's something else. You wouldn't feel reluctant to tell me Morgana Cassidy had tried to get fresh with Tony Raglan. Though unless he looked much different back then, I'm not sure what she saw in him."

I raised an eyebrow. "Compassion, maybe? Not everyone focuses on looks. Anyway, the thing is... she was into divination, all that sort of stuff. Bit of a hippy, though not in a bad way. More the aesthetic, I think. So...Tony Raglan taught her the runes."

I watched that sink in. Mark Roscoe shook his head, whistling between his teeth. "So, this rune symbol at the Claire Jakely scene – it could be Morgana Cassidy trying to get a message to Tony Raglan, yes?"

"It could be." The words felt as though they were being dragged out of me. They left barbed-wire tracks on my tongue.

"Bill...you need to face up to the fact that Morgana Cassidy is probably our killer. We need to start looking for her. We need to speak to Tony Raglan. When's he getting out of hospital?"

"End of the week. They're worried he's got some kind of infection, or something. Apparently his temperature keeps rising, and he's lost a bit of weight."

"Is that really a bad thing?"

I laughed. "I'm guessing it is if they don't know why. And they probably don't want to risk Feroc going to the papers and talking about the quality of hospital food. I think they're just covering their own arses, to be fair. But neither of them will be home before Friday. They'll probably turn them loose then – won't want them in when the drunks and cheating partners start rolling up, after all."

Roscoe laughed. "Tell them to call you when they're ready to be discharged. The call me. We'll go together to pick them up, and we'll talk to Tony Raglan about Morgana Cassidy together. Alright?"

I nodded, and got to my feet. "You'll want her personnel file?"

"Please." I took a notepad and pen from the shelf beside my desk, and scrawled a few lines, giving Detective Inspector Roscoe my permission, as the uniformed Inspector available, if not Morgana Cassidy's Inspector at the time of her employment with Lothing police, the permission he needed to ask for that file. He could have demanded it, anyway – this was a murder enquiry, after all – but we liked to try and do things politely, if we could.

He at least had the grace to look embarrassed. "I'm sorry about this, Bill." I sighed, and held out my hand.

"If you're right – then so am I." We shook silently, solemnly, each watching the other's eyes, and seeing in them an echo of our own soul.

# RAGNAROK

*One week to go.*

One week, Andrew James Jackson, and then your soul will be incarnate no more.

I often wondered about visiting a medium, talking to those I'd killed, asking them what their anti-life was like. Finding out, once and for all, if there was life after death, or if the last thing we ever knew was that we were about to soil ourselves.

As I threaded black ribbon through the hole in the wooden disc that bore the rune *Fehu* – in case Andrew Jackson, when we met for the final time next week, had nothing suitable to tie the runemark to on his person – I wondered about the runes as a divination tool, how they worked, who could use them, and what they could be used for.

Like many people, I'd had my time of getting drunk and playing with a Ouija board – I was still certain that some kind of mechanism was in play, causing the glass to move: it *had* originally been released as a board game, after all – there was bound to be some trick to it – but runes seemed more real, somehow. I couldn't see how you could falsify them, or how someone else could, once you'd learnt the meanings. I wondered if you could teach yourself the runes, the way you could teach yourself tarot? Or was it like Yoga, and, to do it properly, someone who already knew about it had to pass that knowledge on? I'd have a look online, once I'd sorted out Andrew Jackson, and see if there were any rune readers locally. I wouldn't mind learning more about the tool that had become my trademark – it seemed like a professional courtesy, really.

I'd taken the week off work, so that I could dedicate it to tracking Andrew Jackson. The final week of anyone's life was the most important – even if they weren't murdered, their final week often had moments at which their death could have been avoided, or at least postponed.

I'd done the same thing with Claire Jakely, and, to be honest, I was probably going to end up getting sacked. That didn't bother me. A job was just a job, a way to earn money, and there were plenty of ways open to those who knew what they were looking for. Killing, however, was a vocation, a calling – I was not obligated to complete the work, but neither was I free to abandon it.

So, my dreary day job helping overindulged lap dogs of women find the 'perfect' shade of make up, for skin that literally would suit anything, might end up going out the window. I wouldn't be overly upset, although I would miss the 'tricky' customers, as my colleagues called them, the people who *needed* our services, the women whose skin tone simply refused to co-operate with any obvious shade. One woman who came in regularly was clearly transgender: that didn't bother me. I liked the way she was actually receptive to learning about how make up worked, the way she seemed to genuinely value my knowledge and expertise. I liked the fact that she would come in every few weeks, having clearly had to save up before she could ask about the next item she was curious to try. The other women came in whenever they were bored, whenever their child benefit was paid. They were loud and grating and opinionated, and believed they were immediately better than me because I worked in a shop. The transgender woman – Alice, according to the debit card she would hand over – was quiet, reflective, and always careful to pay attention to what I told her, and to ask questions in a way that made it clear she thought of me as an expert.

I liked being thought of as an expert.

Murder, an area in which I was also something of an expert, might be considered an unusual vocation, and certainly it was considered an immoral one, but it wasn't as uncommon a calling as you might think. In 2015, some professor somewhere worked out that there were two active serial killers in the UK in every generation. Bearing in mind that not every killer is a serial killer, and that there are plenty of areas in the UK where a body could remain undiscovered for months, if not years, and that was probably an underestimate. And then, of course, murder, if you became expert at it, wasn't necessarily something you had to retire from. That meant that there could easily be generational overlaps of murderers, with one generation having three or four serial killers active within it.

I was always interested in reports of things like 9/11 and the Grenfell Tower fire, because such happenings were perfect for newly-aware killers. There was already so much carnage, so much assumption of life lost, that, if you got it right, you could kill more or less with impunity. And people caught up in something terrible were always so much more trusting of the motives of strangers than they might otherwise be.

I didn't hijack such events – each killer will have their own personal moral code, and mine was to stay away from people whose lives were in a state of flux. Besides, the kind of people who suffered as a result of instances such as Grenfell weren't my target. They weren't wealthy – they were dead *because of* the wealthy.

I smiled to myself. The Grenfell Tower fire had come at just the right time. I'd wondered, when Claire had been found and identified so promptly, whether it was a sign that I needed to retire, or at least take a sabbatical. Then there was Grenfell, a clarion call, telling me that I needed to avenge these people, that I was their guardian angel.

I doubted Claire Jakely and Andrew Jackson would agree with me. Andrew would laugh at me, while Claire would tell me that I had no right to be co-opting a tragedy for my own perverted agenda. Or at least, she would, if she were still alive, if her own perverted agenda hadn't signed her death warrant.

I had a feeling that this generation would see a larger number of serial killers, and a larger number of murderers generally, because this was a generation in flux, and flux states always encouraged those of us with such ambitions as mine to follow them, wherever they may lead. People were angry, and, under the right – or the wrong, depending on your point of view – circumstances, the white heat of anger could be cooled and forged into a steel-bright rage that would endure for years.

My estimate is that there are at least ten killers – those with a calling to murder – active in the UK. Ten wolves, preying on the sheepish rest of you.

And we won't all show our hand immediately, nor will we all kill in ways that are obvious. Most of us will be caught fairly soon after we begin killing, owing to inexperience or overconfidence, or a lethal cocktail of both. But at least two or three of us will survive, uncaught and unchallenged.

And I was one of them.

## P.C. Tony Raglan
## LB 265

"This must be how the slags we put away feel when they finally get released after their joke of a sentence." I still felt a little spaced out, I was still in a lot of pain, but I was ready to go home. So was Feroc, currently helping me button my shirt – moving my right arm too much still had me doubled over and sobbing. I was sitting on the end of my hospital bed, Feroc was in a wheelchair we'd been assured would only be for a couple of weeks – he was scheduled for daily physiotherapy, which would be done at home by a community physio. Freed up hospital space, saved them transport costs, and made it less likely people wouldn't show up, I suppose. I smiled – Feroc even managed to look good in a wheelchair. If he were straight, he'd be charming girls into his bed with stories of surfing accidents, shark encounters, or dirt-bike racing upsets.

Somehow, telling people the truth – that you were a copper who'd been injured in the line of duty – never had the same effect. Unless they were in the Job, too, of course.

Thinking about that made me think about Morgana, something I'd been doing, off and on, since Wyckham had asked about her. I wondered if she knew I'd been shot. I wondered, if she did know, if she remembered me? If she cared? She'd promised that she wouldn't forget me, had promised that she'd always be thinking of me, but that, as they say, was long ago and far away. She'd fallen far from grace since those words were spoken: the promise had been made before the killings began. Perhaps the Morgana Cassidy that existed now wasn't the same woman who'd spoken to me on that windswept London street all those years ago. Even to me, it seemed like a lifetime ago – how must it seem to her, in her madness?

"There," Feroc looked up, smiling. "All smart and ready to meet the boss."

"I'm assuming they'll let us know when he's here?"

As if on cue, Sonia's mop of curly hair appeared around the edge of the door. "Gentlemen – your carriage awaits. Come on, out you get – I'm sure you've heard we're at crisis point."

"You shouldn't hassle us, you know – I mean, Tony here's basically Jesus – stabbed through the side, and all that."

Sonia raised an eyebrow. "Yeah? You ever get nailed so hard you didn't get up for three days?"

I grinned. "Wouldn't you like to know? Anyway – not my pantheon, though he does sound like a bloke who had his head screwed on. And I have to applaud anyone who horsewhips bankers, really."

"Camel-whips."

"You what?"

"Camel-whips," Feroc repeated. "They wouldn't've had horses in Israel at that time. Well, actually, they wouldn't've had Israel, at that time. Or at least it wouldn't have been a country."

"How do you know all of this?" I slowly got to my feet as Sonia grabbed Feroc's latest accessory, spun him round, and wheeled him into the corridor. My left leg seemed to drag, and I had no idea why.

"I actually listened in History. And read the Bible. 'Israel', in Biblical times, would have been a relatively small area of land, settled by a small tribe and their descendants."

"And then we cocked everything up after the second World War," I commented. Sonia rolled her eyes as she rolled Feroc into the lift.

"Ain't that just all history, all the time? White British people cocked up – the end."

"That's racist." I was laughing. "I could report you for that."

"It's not racist if it's true. But, y'know, if you're upset, I could probably arrange a safe space for you – the Falkland Islands should just about be big enough."

I never wanted to lose Feroc, or Sonia. I never wanted to not have someone who could reliably take me out of myself, out of whatever situation I happened to be in, and make me laugh. Even though laughing hurt, it felt good. Painful, but good. That probably made me some kind of masochist, but it was the truth.

As the lift made its slow way down, Feroc turned to me.
"What do you think about the Christian god?"
I raised an eyebrow, but gave him an answer. "I think, if people
believe in Him, that's their business. They should leave everyone
else to theirs, and be afforded the same courtesy. "
"You don't agree with Stephen Fry, then? That there can't be a
compassionate god, because kids die of cancer, they get abused,
all that sort of thing?"
The lift ground to a halt. I waited for the doors to open, waited
until we were out in the expanse of the reception area.
"Why children, especially? Adults get cancer. Adults are abused.
It's just as bad, when you're on the receiving end, however old you
are."
Sonia parked Feroc at the end of a row of plastic chairs. I sat
down beside him. "Your boss should be here soon. Fascinating as
your conversation is, I'll leave you to it – some of us have work to
do."
Feroc watched her walk off, then turned to me.
"You don't think it's different, when bad things happen to kids?
Worse, somehow?"
"No, I don't. Life can be crap. It's part of the deal – you can't have
the wonder without the worry. Life is only precious because it's
fragile and finite. We can be hurt, broken, and, one day, we will
cease to exist. And everyone who claimed they loved us will dry
their tears, and move on with their life." I sighed, and closed my
eyes. "The problem is, Feroc, when you believe that bad things
*shouldn't* happen to children, you're a very small step away from
believing that they *don't* happen to children. It becomes almost
imperative for your brain to *tell you* that nothing bad happens to
children." I turned to look at Feroc. "You haven't arrested a nonce,
yet, have you?"
"No."
"I have. Too many times. You know the one thing they all have in
common, besides being the lowest kind of slag?"
"What?" It was a whisper.
"They all believe they didn't do anything wrong. Not the way a

thief or a con-man tries to swing it that he didn't do anything wrong, because he feels obliged to argue the toss, like it's part of some game – the nonces genuinely don't see that what they did was wrong. They'll talk about how much they love children, how precious children are, how beautiful, how they should be looked after and cherished. They genuinely believe that what they're doing is a part of love." I grimaced, grinding my eyelids into the sockets to try and black out the reality of what I was about to say. "And it is."

"It's abuse!" Feroc flushed scarlet, whether from embarrassment or anger I couldn't tell, as several people glanced in our direction.

"Yes, it is," I replied, calmly, slowly opening my eyes. "But it's a kind of love, too – love always has the potential to turn to abuse."

Feroc shook his head. "I don't believe that. I won't believe it. How can you say that, when you've told me you love me?"

"Because I am aware that I have the ability to behave abusively towards you. I choose not to, but that choice requires an acceptance that I can do things to you which are wrong. It requires an acceptance that bad things can happen to you." I paused, and let the silence speak for a moment. Somewhere, a clock ticked too loudly. "Do you understand, now? Do you see why it's so dangerous to get caught up in being outraged about bad things happening to children, particularly?"

Feroc's voice, when he answered, was quiet. Afraid.

"I don't think I can ever understand." He wouldn't look at me.

I closed my eyes again. "Then let me put it this way: one time, I'd arrested this nonce – a real sicko. And he calmly turned to me, and said, in this upper-class, public-school voice: 'But, Officer – this is no different to someone being homosexual. That was deemed unlawful, once, but is no longer.' That spun me for a fucking loop, Feroc – because it was true. If I had no choice in my attractions, then how could I believe these men had a choice in theirs? Men like me had loved one another against the law for decades, centuries – how was paedophilia any different?"

"But it is different – surely you know that? Surely you didn't let some nonce drag you down that particular rabbit hole?"

I sighed. "No, I didn't. And yes, I know it's different. But the only difference is, we're equals. And I don't just mean we're both adults. I mean we're both working full time. We're both being paid a living wage, however much we might whine about it being otherwise. We're both white. We're both able-bodied, usually. Neither of us has mental health issues, or learning disabilities. We're true equals, you and I, in that either one of us could call it quits and walk out tomorrow, and be able to take care of himself. Love – any love – is abusive where the partners involved are not equals. Even if the equality is only that one partner earns less than the other, there's still the potential for abuse."

The automatic doors hissed open, and I saw Bill Wyckham and Mark Roscoe step through. I wondered, briefly, why they'd both come.

Feroc shook his head, glancing in their direction as I struggled to my feet, suddenly feeling my age. "I don't believe you, " he said, calmly. "I won't ever believe that the world is as bleak as you try and paint it."

"You'll learn, one day. In twenty years' time, you'll understand that I'm not trying to paint the world any colour that's not already there. Alright, Guv – don't worry about the wheels – they assure me it's not permanent."

Wyckham laughed. "With you around, it'd better not be. How're you going to manage, with your arm?" He nodded to the sling that supported my right arm – it wasn't broken, but it had been a pretty close call. I struggled to move it, broken bones or not.

I waved my left hand. "We'll manage, somehow. It's alright – Feroc's sister's moving in, just until he's fully fit again."

"That should be fun for you. You met her before?"

"We've spoken on the phone. She seems nice."

"Well, that's a start." Wyckham grabbed the wheelchair, and we headed out into the damp, drizzle-threatening air.

## P.C. Feroc Hanson
## LB 599

As I sat beside the DI, watching his hands on the wheel – hands that were so utterly unlike Tony's, and as I half-listened to the Inspector talking to Tony, who had somehow managed to fit reasonably comfortably into the back of what was, at the end of the day, a fairly small car, I thought about the conversation Tony and I had just had.

I didn't agree with him, not in the slightest, but he did make a certain kind of sense. A depressing kind of sense, but sense nonetheless. I sighed. Sometimes, having been brought up by parents who valued intellectual debate, and who believed that disagreeing with someone was no reason to dislike them, was a pain. I wanted to be able to refuse to have anything to do with Tony and his difficult, disturbing views – but that ship had sailed two years or more ago. Whatever brand of madness led him down the dark alleys I sometimes glimpsed in his mind, I was tied to it, now.

That thought should probably scare me a lot more than it did, but a lack of fear around potential insanity, and certainly around unsettling points of view, was one of the upsides of being raised by intelligent, thoughtful parents. As my father had explained to me, when he'd brought me a translated copy of *Mein Kampf* to read: "They're only another person's thoughts, and another person's thoughts can't hurt you. True, they can lead people to take actions that are very damaging indeed, as Hitler's thoughts did, but they can't corrupt your own mind. It's important that you know what people with whom you disagree think, or thought, when they were still living, because if you know what people are thinking, you can challenge their thinking, and perhaps dissuade them from a potentially damaging course of action. If you shut yourself away, and refuse to allow yourself knowledge of their thoughts, if you fear those thoughts – then they've already won."

I hoped Dad would come and visit while I was off sick – I had a feeling he and Tony would get on well, and have a lot to talk about. I would say 'argue about', but my Dad didn't argue – he talked. Calmly, respectfully, and always with full attention paid to the person with whom he was talking. Even if they started shouting and becoming emotional, my father never did. It had won him a lot of friends, even among those who didn't share his liberal, tolerant, pretty much socialist views, and it meant he could have very intense conversations on social media without anyone ever once becoming abusive. Although that wasn't quite true – someone had once told my Dad that "your bleeding heart should be ripped out of your spineless chest, and thrown to the wolves you refuse to believe are at the door!" My father had calmly typed back: "Very well – wolves, also, must eat, whether I believe in their presence at my door or not. Although my heart my not be to their taste." I'd been one of over thirty people to click "Like" on that.

I'd been surprised by my Dad's enthusiasm for social media, and surprised again when, discussing it with Tony, I'd discovered that he shared my Dad's view that social media, far from being a barrier to people engaging with one another, actually encouraged them to do so.

"Think about it – all these people moaning that no one ever talks to anyone any more: we never talked to each other anyway! We muttered hello in passing, we argued about cricket, we commented on the blindingly obvious, briefly, and then we turned back to our paper and our pint, and spent the rest of the day in sullen silence. You watch people on line, and literally all they're doing, all the time, is talking. Even when they're just sharing daft pictures, that's a form of talking – it's the same way we'd tell a joke, only everyone can join in. Even people you don't know."

I let my attention drift from my own thoughts to the conversation going on in the back seat, my ears pricking up as I heard the name 'Morgana'. Wyckham had asked about Morgana before, when he'd dropped in to check how we were doing shortly after the accident. It was clearly someone Tony knew, and Wyckham was clearly anxious to talk to her. I got the feeling, though, that Tony didn't know as much as the Inspector hoped he did.

"Tony – do you ever hear from Morgana? Things...seem to have gone quiet, with her."

"I'd noticed. But no, she hasn't been in touch."

"She's alright, though?"

"I don't know, Guv. The way things were, I don't think anyone can ever really be alright after something like that, y'know?"

"I know, Tony. Believe me, I know. We screwed up."

"Yeah. You did, Guv. Everyone else, I mean, not just you, personally. No one listened to me."

"I know."

"Do you, though?" Tony sounded pained. I focused on the conversation – the DI seemed to be listening in, too. "Because you know what? I don't think I could trust that I'd be listened to if there was a next time."

There was a long pause. It was the DI who broke it. "But, if it's feasible, you'd go undercover for me, right?"

"What?!"

"Hush, Fer – I'll talk about it later, okay? Yes, Guv – because I can get myself out of a situation, if I need to. Morgana wasn't experienced enough. She shouldn't have been sent undercover."

"I wasn't there, Raglan. I didn't send her."

"No, I know that. But you hesitated about bringing Connor out, didn't you? CID are all the same – you always want more, and uniform are always the ones who have to bleed for you to get it."

"That's uncalled for, and unfair, Raglan."

"Is it?"

The silence slapped back into place. I could almost see its smirk. "If we'd brought Connor out, you might well be dead." The DI's voice was low, flat, and deadly. Everyone recoiled from it.

"Don't you *dare* try and shut me down with that." Tony's voice was all razor blades and broken glass. I could almost taste the blood he wanted to spill. "Don't you *ever* try and silence me with the shame of me still being alive. Guv." He bit off the last word. In the rear view mirror, I could see the fire dancing in his eyes. He had been to hell and back, since the accident on the bridge, and he was dangerously close to the edge. I wondered if the DI realised that.

Clearly, he did – or at least sensed that he needed to back off. "Am I dropping you off home, then, or are you needed at the nick?"

"Drop them home, Mark. And me with them. When you get back to the factory, send one of the van boys out to mine, have them bring the bloody parrot back. I'll call the girls, warn them they'll have to say goodbye."

"I'll need to talk to Raglan, Bill."

"I'm right here, Guv – you don't need to act like I'm deaf, or an imbecile."

"I think you've said more than enough for now, Mark. We'll talk, us two, when I get back to the nick. In the meantime, I'm going to try and undo the damage you've done -"

"The damage *I've* done! You know, maybe if your boy there had taken one for the team and got his leg over, Morgana Cassidy wouldn't've gone crazy on us."

Suddenly, everyone was shouting. I joined in, even though I hadn't got a clue what anyone was talking about. Finally, beautifully, Wyckham's voice rose above it all.

"That's enough, Mark. Tony's literally just out of hospital."

"So?!" Roscoe was nearly screaming, now. "What's the worst we can do? Put him back there?"

The sound of the slap I gave my Detective Inspector echoed through the car like a door slamming shut on eternity.

It stopped the shouting, though.

## Inspector Bill Wyckham
## LB 81

"It's Valley Transport. They'll be with you about five. No – I thought the neighbours might get a bit upset, seeing a police van twice in a relatively short space of time. Yep, yep, love you too. She wants a what? No. Look - look, tell her to read up about them. We'll go to the zoo or something, somewhere they have a lot of them. An aviary, or something. Maybe she can have a budgie, get a feel for things with something manageable."

I ended the call, and looked up, careful not to meet anyone's gaze. "Idaho should be back with you just after five. " Silence. I sighed. "Look, Hanson, what you did -"

"You going to suspend me, Sir?"

"No. You know I'm not. What would be the point? You're on medical leave for as long as a suspension would last."

"You going to write me up? Insubordination, isn't it?"

"Detective Inspector Roscoe was out of order. I'll tell that as often as it needs to be told, to anyone and everyone who needs to hear it." I turned to face Tony Raglan, who was slowly, and, it seemed, painfully, playing Solitaire. "We do need to talk about Morgana, though."

"Nothing to say. The Force screwed up, she got destroyed, and now she's gone."

"But is she, Tony? Is she as gone as everyone thinks, or is there something you're not telling us?" I sighed. "Look, Tony, it looks bad. We've got a female killer, more than likely, and we can't get a trace on a woman we know has killed before."

Tony turned a card over, swore, and picked up the TV remote. The theme tune for *Countdown* came on.

"Look, Tony -"

"D'you mind, Sir? Only, I'm not on duty, and I'm watching this."

"Tony – we need to talk about Morgana."

"I don't even know who she is, Tony – what was Roscoe on about, in the car?"

Feroc had been out if when I'd spoken with Tony at the hospital –

it was the only reason I'd felt able to.

I watched Tony. His shoulders stiffened, and he sat, staring deliberately, intently, at the television screen.

"Tony?" Feroc's voice was soft, gentle, like someone trying to call a frightened kitten. "It's alright – I won't be angry. But I do want you to tell me."

"I want to watch this, first."

So we sat and watched *Countdown* together, as though we were old folk in a nursing home. I made Feroc tea, and Tony coffee, during the commercial break. Tony surprised me by beating all of the contestants in each of the numbers rounds, and Feroc confirmed his intelligence by not only excelling at the letters rounds, but also getting the Conundrum within ten seconds. It was clear the only reason he didn't attempt to answer the numbers questions was because it mattered to him that Tony got to enjoy being good at something that required intellectual ability.

I remembered, a long time ago, being involved in a lively debate about whether gay men could ever actually experience love, in the purest, non-sexual sense. Seeing Feroc quietly step aside, without even seeming to do so, so that his partner could feel good about himself, told me that they definitely could, and did – and were perhaps better at it than the rest of us.

Finally, Tony looked up. "So. Morgana. What do you want to know? Feroc?"

"Who was she, and what did Roscoe mean, in the car, when he talked about you taking one for the team?"

Tony sighed, and closed his eyes. He looked exhausted, and my heart broke for him. He shouldn't have to go through this. Mark Roscoe should have kept his mouth shut.

"Morgana Cassidy was a copper. A good copper. One of the best. She was passionate, caring, and bold as a pack of fox cubs. There was nothing she wouldn't do, and it didn't come from wanting to prove she was as good as a bloke – she knew she was as good as any one of us, and better than more than a few." Tony's voice became rough, as though he was speaking over sandpaper. "She wanted to be an Area driver. She'd've made a good one – perhaps even better than me. She had the common sense to know when to call it a day – it was innate, with her. I... I had to learn it. Am still having to learn it. I don't think I'll ever really get it. She would have been so bloody good, behind the wheel. But she went undercover, instead – that job came up a week before the next driving course. And she took that, instead of putting in her papers. Because it was for CID, and everyone's been brainwashed into thinking CID is the be all and end all." He took a deep breath, and I saw the spasm of pain that flashed across his face. He was fighting against some powerful emotions, maybe even a few demons, and I wondered if he'd have the strength to survive. "She was bait for a group of perverts. Rapists, nonces, human traffickers. Heavy-duty stuff that she wasn't even close to being experienced enough for. She asked for me as one of her handlers – that shattered every precedent, having a uniform as a handler for a UC, but she said she wouldn't do the job if I wasn't involved. I wish they'd refused. I wish she'd been told no, and made to do the bloody Area course, instead. But she wasn't. I was assigned, along with a CID officer. She went in – and she didn't come out again. Not really. I could see she was cracking up, could see she couldn't take the pressure, but I was just a plod. No one listened to me. I was too bloody scared of the brass to go and break her out of there myself. I cared more about my job than her."

"And what Roscoe said?"

Tony opened his eyes, and I was stunned to see he was close to tears. He made no effort to wipe them away. He didn't even blink. His voice was flat, his face, beyond the tears, expressionless. "She had a crush on me. That was how I got access to her, as her handler – I pretended to be her boyfriend. Nah, mate, I don't mind she's working for you – less hassle than having the neighbours nosing about in my business, know what I mean? She being good, is she? Give me five minutes with her, in private, know what I mean? Wink, wink, nudge, nudge. " He sighed, and the tears began to fall. "She wanted me to sleep with her. Looking back, long after it was far too late, I realised she'd thought she might get pregnant, and have an automatic out. But I baulked. I freaked out.

I told her I was gay. Told her about Max." Tears were streaming down his face, now. "Two months later, she begged us to get her out. Two months later, I was suspended after I slapped the DI who'd sent her in, because he refused, said she needed to be in 'just a few weeks longer.' There was apparently some big influx of trafficked kids due to arrive, and of course he was on the scent, tail up. He wanted to be there, to take the glory." Tony gave a soft moan – I don't think he was conscious of doing so – and closed his eyes, tears still falling. "Two weeks later, the house she was in burned to the ground. We found a tarot card – the Empress – with Morgana's shoulder number on. At first, we thought it was a message from the gang, telling us they'd realised what she was...but then the post mortems happened."

I knew the story, and closed my eyes against the knowledge. Feroc didn't. "And?"

"And, every single man – and it was only men, even though there'd been a dozen women and at least ten kids in that house – every man had been brutally stabbed, before the fire started. There was blood, on the tarot card – we'd thought it was Morgana's." He paused, swallowing hard. "It wasn't. The lab identified at least six different blood types. All male. Morgana had killed those men. She'd stabbed them in a frenzy, and she and the women and children were gone." Tony opened his eyes on a sigh. "They turned up, in time, one or two at a time. The other women, the children. Some as victims of other predators, some as desperate criminals, some just handing themselves in, lost and afraid. Morgana was never among them. She was gone. I went looking for her..." He broke off, and looked at me. "Eventually, I found her. No one knew that. I've never told anyone. She was in a state, but she wasn't a killer. Not then. I don't count the men at the house – they were scum, and she was desperate. She wasn't insane, but she was on the edge. I stayed with her – for almost a week, I stayed with her. She was living on the streets, in the East End. I used to walk to Harrods, every day – there and back, in the evening, after they'd closed. I'd take the food they'd thrown away – I know it's theft, technically, but that didn't matter, not then:

somehow, it mattered to me that she had nice food, expensive food, the kind of stuff neither of us would ever have been able to afford. I took what I could from their skips. In the morning, I'd go to M&S, buy enough for both of us. I used to sit there, in the doorway where she was sleeping, at night, and watch her eat whatever I'd managed to get that day. It was important that she ate more than enough, because one day, I knew I'd have to come back, and she needed to have something in reserve, to see her through."

I didn't know how far it was from whatever part of the East End Morgana Cassidy had fetched up in to Knightsbridge, but, if Tony Raglan had been walking that, even if it was only a mile each way, every day for two weeks, and not eating much, if anything, himself, the state he'd been in when he'd come back made a terrible, agonising sense. He met my gaze, and smiled sadly. "It's alright, Guv – I made sure I had a sandwich, a cup of coffee. I had to stay with it, to look after Morgana." He sighed, the tears beginning to fall more heavily. "And then I had to come home. And two days later, I heard about the first murder." He was sobbing, now, yelping a little as the movement jerked his injured arm. Feroc looked pained, unable to get up and go to him. Slowly, Tony brought himself back under control, and looked up, "That was my fault, too. She'd told me, when I'd asked if she'd be alright, once I left, that she'd be fine – 'I'll find other people like those scum back home, and kill them. That kind always have money. I'll still be able to eat from Harrods.' I laughed – she didn't. I should have realised she was serious. But I didn't. I got on a train, came home, and set about putting my poxy life back together. I abandoned her. I let her down – again. I made her what she is."

He lifted his head, staring blankly at me. "What's this about a female killer, Guv?"

"Like I told you in the hospital – the old dear you were chasing was pretty sure she'd seen a murder being committed. And she described a woman was the killer."

"She described Morgana Cassidy?"

"Well, no, but -"

"No. Of course she didn't. Because Morgana wouldn't – hang on. There haven't been murders with Morgana's mark for...eighteen months? Longer? I'd've known, if there had been, and there haven't. What's brought this on, this idea that just because a woman killed someone, it's Morgana Cassidy?"

My voice was soft. "You taught her the runes, didn't you?"

"Yes – what's that got to … Roscoe. Roscoe asked me about a runemark. *Fehu.* He told me … No. No, Morgana wouldn't do that. And anyway, when I taught her the runes, I gave her her own set – I'd found them in a charity shop, of all places. Welsh slate. They were her runes, I knew that then. If she were killing, if she were trying to contact me through the runes, she'd have left a rune from her set."

"Assuming she still has it with her."

"She will do. It's a way for her to make money. People pay for runecasts, tarot readings. She had a tarot deck, too – other than...well, other than the one we saw cards from. She kept them well away from where anyone could get to them easily. The cards and the runes."

"All the same..."

"No. This isn't Morgana. I'd have seen her by now, if it was."

I looked at Tony. "What do you mean?"

"Nothing."

"Tony -"

"I just – I would have seen something of her, in the runemark the DI showed me. That's all I meant. It was handwritten – I'd have seen something of her in it."

"It was a few plain lines."

"I would have still known if she'd drawn it, just as I could tell you within seconds which copper in the nick had written my name on a piece of paper."

I smiled. Tony wasn't lying – he could never be the one to pull answers out of a hat, because, even through multiple folds, in shadowed outline, he could easily and accurately identify block capital writing.

"I believe you. But Roscoe doesn't."

With an effort, Tony got to his feet, and crossed the room to sit beside Feroc.

"Then convince him, Guv. You're on my side, right? Bring the DI round."

I shook my head sadly. "I'm afraid that's going to be your job." I glanced at my watch. Gone four o'clock – we'd been talking for well over an hour. "Let me make you two something to eat – you must be starving. Have you even got anything in?" I realised they probably hadn't – who arranged for grocery shopping to be done when they were in hospital, for crying out loud? "I'll do a quick blitz round the shop at the end of the road – they good for groceries?"

"Yeah. Prices aren't a rip off, either."

"Right. Any requests? By the time I've done that and sorted you something half decent – any objections if I do you a ham and cheese omelet with salad? Tony, don't give me that look – you have to eat vegetables sometimes. They're good for you. God, it's like talking to a toddler with you, isn't it? So, other than Mr 'Help, I Can't Cope With Green Stuff', you're both fine with that? Good. Anyway, as I was saying, by the time I've sorted that, your bloody parrot should be on his way back. I'll pick up enough stuff for a week, things that don't need a lot of cooking. When's your sister getting here, Feroc?"

"Tomorrow, Guv. She's got to work late today, but she's leaving first thing."

"Right – I'll give my missus a ring. You'll have me for company until she gets here. Someone's got to keep you two out of trouble."

# RAGNAROK

*Well, Mr. Jackson – we seem to have arrived at the point of no
return. Or, at least, at your point of no return. From this day
forward, there will be one less Andrew Jackson in the world, and
for all your arrogant pretensions, for all your conceit, for all your
wealth, no one will actually care.*

We are never truly missed. People are shocked, they are upset,
briefly, and then they move on. They forget. Their lives, always so
much more important, consume them once again.

Grief doesn't last. It isn't enduring. It's weather, passing through, a
temporary disturbance in the force and focus of the everyday. We
believe people will care because we believe we matter. We don't.
No one does, in the end.

It's why I can't accept that murder, when done with style and from
a sense of calling or vocation, is wrong. We don't matter. Our lives
don't matter.

Andrew Jackson's life certainly didn't matter, and soon – mere
hours, now – it would no longer even exist. Andrew Jackson,
murder victim, late of this parish.

I would need to start looking for another victim. Male, I thought,
and in his twilight years. I would not kill children – the children of
the wealthy are not to blame. Sometimes, I see children being
rewarded with obscene wealth for very little reason, but, again,
their parents are usually the driving force behind things. Besides,
killing children tends to bring down a much more intense and
blood-lusting focus from the powers that be. Society does not
tolerate bad things happening to children. Only the government is
permitted to defile innocence.

I should have started looking for my next victim before now. I
was getting slack, and slackness led to mistakes.

But I would make no mistakes with Andrew Jackson. His death
would be a testament to commitment, to calling, to dedication to
the learning of a craft.

I sat in my taxi – not recognised by any of the local licensing
authorities, and only a taxi periodically – outside the town's

railway station, blending in with the other hungry hopefuls on the rank, for now. I glanced at my watch. Twenty minutes, if his train was on time. I knew he'd come to me, to my car, out of all the others here – because I would be offering something none of the other drivers were.

For a start, when I was leaning casually against the sleek black of my car, the soft grey of my pinstripe suit and the white of my cheekily unbuttoned blouse contrasting elegantly against the paintwork, I looked ready for work, something few of the male drivers managed even when someone was right beside their car, waiting for them to look up from their tabloids. And I looked like the business people who hired me, and who almost always took a card, with the mobile number that went to a pay as you go phone that wasn't my regular mobile. Of course, with Claire Jakely, I'd had to retrieve the card – that's why I'd only just been leaving the alley when the old woman in the Escort had pulled up across the road.

It was a stupid mistake, an amateur's mistake, and one I would not allow to happen again.

20.50. Eight minutes. How swift can be the ending of a life.

After this, after Andrew, I would have a short holiday somewhere, the kind of area, the kind of hotel, that successful entrepreneurs might frequent.

*Business or pleasure, Madam?*
Oh, a little of both, I rather think.

I saw the lights of the train in the distance, and got out of the car, sprawling, smiling, waiting.

## P.C. Feroc Hanson
### LB 599

I sat in silence for a long time after Tony had finished speaking. Bill Wyckham called his wife to say he wouldn't be home tonight, that he'd come home once he knew my sister was going to be able to manage "these two rogues." He left to go to the corner shop. He came back. I could hear him, sorting out something to do with food in the kitchen, talking to himself.

I felt exhausted, having heard all that Tony had had to say about Morgana, and what had happened with her. I wondered how he felt, having to tell it. It must have been like living through it, all over again, and still without the hope of a different ending.

It sounded like this undercover op had been a cock up from the start. Clearly there was some inherent vulnerability in Morgana that had been triggered by the things she'd seen in that house. Clearly, the operation itself had called for a far more experienced officer, and, perhaps, a handler who would have been able to make his voice heard, in the way Tony, being "nothing but a Plod", as far as CID were concerned, fatally hadn't. I wondered what the grooming for undercover work had been like? Surely, if there were risk factors around Morgana Cassidy, they should have been picked up long before the prospect of the operation was even mentioned to her? Maybe they had been, and, like Tony's later concerns, had been ignored.

An officer – vulnerable because of her gender, because women in male-dominated spaces will always be vulnerable – had been placed in a situation for which she was manifestly unprepared. When she had reached out, had asked to come home, the desire for a result had been put ahead of her welfare.

That was unforgivable. One of the concepts that you first encountered at basic training, and that solidified itself in your mind as your service progressed, was that the Force was a pack, that it was in the world, but most definitely not of the world. There was Us – the Job, the Force, Her Majesty's Oiks, as Tony would say – and Them: everybody else, the scum and the slag and

Joe Public and the politicians and all the rest.

We weren't like them, and they didn't like us – not even the law-abiding ones. All we had, in this world we policed, without its consent and without, for the most part, its welcome, was each other, the Family of the Force. And the trust, the total, whole-hearted trust in one another, in every other Blue. We formed bonds quickly, sometimes very intense bonds. Being let down by another officer was widely believed to be as bad, as damaging, as soul-destroying, as being let down by your spouse. More so, in many cases – coppers often weren't very good at marriage, especially if they'd married outside the uniform. That eternal sense of otherness, again. A non-Blue could never understand us: we'd always be speaking a different language, shouting at each other in the dark.

Actually, that was closer to the truth: when a copper tried to sustain a relationship with someone outside the Job, it was like someone shouting at a deaf person in the dark. Crass, disrespectful, and with no chance of going anywhere.

And yet Tony had managed it, first with Max, and then, in a different way, with Steve Lassiter. I assumed there would have been other relationships, before Max, and that, since his sexuality had come as a surprise to his colleagues, they had also been with people far outside our circle.

It hadn't just been Morgana Cassidy who'd been hurt. As Bill Wyckham brought plates of omelet and salad through, I looked at Tony, and saw the scars, still there, traced outlines on his face.

He felt he'd failed Morgana Cassidy, and perhaps he had. After all, an intelligent young woman with a bright future in front of her was now a mentally disturbed murderer – or, at least mentally disturbed. There was no proof, not in anything I'd heard, that Morgana Cassidy *was* a killer. A lot of evidence that, yes, strongly suggested the possibility, but nothing concrete. I wondered why nobody seemed to have picked up on that. Was there something else, something that people knew but weren't telling, that made them feel safe in damning one of their own on circumstantial grounds?

A knock at the door startled me out of my reverie: Idaho was home.

Tony was on his feet, a smile breaking through the weariness. As soon as he opened the door, I could hear Idaho's furious joy – he must have still been inside the van – he sounded distant, and I couldn't see his cage. Tony stepped outside, and, a moment later, the air was torn apart with the sound of a very happy, very loud, African Grey parrot screaming the name of everyone he'd ever known and loved, interspersed with characters from *The Big Bang Theory,* over and over again.

Wyckham went over to help the transport driver lift the cage through the door, and set it in its rightful place. Idaho was hanging upside down, his reptilian eyes roving, flapping and squawking delightedly.

The transport driver and his colleague said their goodbyes – Idaho was good at winning hearts, Wyckham's threats of roasting him with a rosemary and thyme dressing not withstanding, and he'd clearly charmed these two on his short journey.

The door closed behind them, and the three of us smiled at each other, and then settled to watch the parrot.

Bill Wyckham, sorting out more drinks in the kitchen, didn't see Tony place his uneaten salad in Idaho's dish – but he clearly heard the "Bad boy! Bad!" - his head appeared round the doorway. "Who's bad?" He glared at Tony. "Did you actually eat your salad, Raglan?" Tony was in the middle of assuring the Inspector that of course he had, he wasn't a complete caveman, when Idaho stepped up onto his perch, making a show of rolling a tomato quarter around his beak.

"What am I going to do with you, Raglan?" Wyckham sighed, and retreated to the kitchen, and the relative simplicity of the washing up.

# RAGNAROK

My smile broadened as he approached, and he showed teeth, matching the gesture.

"You for hire, sweetheart?"

"The car is. As for the body... well, that depends on whether you're a good boy during the ride, doesn't it? Where am I taking you?"

He'd already picked up and pocketed a card, and, winking, responded: "Wherever you like. It's Friday night – I don't have anywhere to be, and I haven't had fun all week."

"Oh, that's a shame. I don't think I've seen you before today?" I knew why that was, of course. I knew everything about Andrew Jackson, including the things he didn't want to tell people.

"No – I stay in London during the week. My company's got a flat. I haven't actually been back for a few weeks – things are a lot more exciting there. But it's quiet right now, and, besides, I need to reassure the chav scum that the big beast still rules the jungle."

He flashed those teeth again, and I kept my own smile from showing just how pathetic I thought he was.

He reached out a hand, fingering the pearls I wore at my throat. I'd been counting on the fact that he would. "Are those real?"

"Would you like a closer look?" I tilted my head, baring my neck, pearls and all, to his gaze, giving an appearance of vulnerability that was very far from my reality. His smile broadened into a smirk.

"Oh, I think there's a lot I'd like to get a closer look a – wha – AGGGHHHH! NOOOAGHH!! Gahk..."

*Pearls before swine,* I thought, as with one swift, practised move, I slid the pearls from my throat around his, and yanked. Harder. Adjusted the angle a little. Yanked. Yanked. And stopped.

Behind the Alfa Romeo's tinted windows, Andrew Jackson slumped forward, red-tinged phlegm bubbling at his lips.

I drew the pearls back, checked the triple-braided copper wire I'd spent hours restringing them onto, tying off each individual pearl either side, so that the strand should break, and replaced them around my own throat, feeling the thrill of the warmth that had so recently, and so abruptly, left the carotid artery region of my dearly departed passenger.

"Well, Andrew," I chirruped, saccharine-sweet and child-bright. "It's a lovely evening for a walk in the woods, don't you think? We should make a move, though – the light won't last."

I wiped the mess from Andrew Jackson's mouth, frowning at the obnoxious stench of the dead, and drove off. If anyone had been able to glance through the Alfa's tinted windscreen, they would have seen a smart, professional woman driving a slumbering man, presumably home.

Well, Andrew Jackson *was* going home: he was going to whatever eternal home he believed awaited him.

## Doug Ferguson
## Taxi Driver

"Look, I'm not sure whether I'm doing the right thing – I don't want to waste your time. I might be jumping the gun. I mean, I don't know anything, right? Times are tough, I get that, we've all got to make a living, right? You can't tell what's going on with someone just from looking at them, can you?"

The copper tried hard not to sigh. I was rambling, I knew that. I probably shouldn't've bothered. It was probably nothing. My mother had always gone on about me the same sort of thing:

*You've got a good brain in your head, Dougie, but no one will ever know about it, because you waffle on and on and on.*

"Sorry, I'm not making a lot of sense. It's just one of the other drivers, another cabbie... well, there's something a bit off about her, right?" I took a deep breath, feeling a bit daft for what I was about to say. "She's too smart, if that makes sense? And her car's too classy...I...well, I think she might be a prostitute."

The copper looked up. "You think this woman is offering sexual favours as well as transport, sir?"

"Yes. I suppose so."

"And other than the fact that she's well presented, and has a smart car, what evidenced do you have to support these suspicions?"

I licked my lips. "Well, she's always chatty with the male punters. I mean, we all chat a bit, it's part of getting repeat business, sometimes, you know? But she seems to focus exclusively on the blokes. And the kind of clothes she wears...well, they'd be uncomfortable over a ten or twelve hour day sitting behind the wheel. And once she's taken a fare, she doesn't seem to come back to the rank."

The copper looked up, This had caught her interest.

"What rank is this?"

"The station. The train station. Most of the runs from there are no more than 20minutes, half an hour max. Commuters coming home, tourists trying to get to their hotels. You go out, you come back, repeat until the last train's in. Then, if you haven't made what you were hoping for, you might drive around the pubs and clubs, try and get a few more coins in your pocket."

"But she doesn't?"

I shook my head. "Not that I've seen, no."

"What kind of car does she drive? You mentioned it seems unusual for a taxicab?"

"A black Alfa Romeo. And there's hardly any advertising on it. Hardly any signage, like."

I took out my phone, and scrolled through the photos until I found the one I was looking for. "I took this last night, when I decided...well, when I decided to come to you with this."

The photo showed the woman leaning against the car, blouse seductively unbuttoned, suit jacket clinging to her curves, the car gleaming, a grinning businessman walking towards her.

The copper studied the photo, and clicked to send it to her own mobile. "Thank you, sir – that's very helpful."

"If it's nothing...if I'm wrong... Look, I don't want to make trouble for someone if I've read things out of order -"

"If the woman in question isn't doing anything illegal, she'll have nothing to worry about. And, in either case, she won't know that you said anything."

"That's good. I mean -"

"I understand, sir. And don't worry – you've done the right thing."

"I hope so."

## RAGNAROK

"Here we are, sir, your stop, I believe. Your *final* stop."

I giggled to myself, glancing round as I got out of the car and crossed to the boot.

Forensic suit, pale blue, because it was less noticeable in the dimming light than the stark white version. Gloves, two pairs of thick vinyl, one worn over the other, topped with a pair of leather bikers' gloves. Court shoes exchanged for black trainers, a cheap, generic pair purchased from the bargain basement store in town, paid in cash. Heavy duty black tarpaulin, and, last but not least, *Fehu* on its black ribbon, ready to be wrapped neatly around Andrew Jackson's tie.

The wood looked good against the pale mauve silk, the ribbon setting then pairing off nicely. Who the hell wore a mauve tie with a cobalt suit? Some people would have killed Andrew Jackson just for that. And a black shirt – he clearly thought he looked edgily fashionable. He just looked like a prat.

Wrap up, carry out – or, rather, wrap up and drag behind me, hoping I didn't meet some fitness fanatic of Fido-lover out for the evening air.

I didn't mess about. I headed straight for the copse of trees I'd identified three weeks previously, where I'd dug a shallow grave, covered over with bracken and leaves until now. Until it was needed.

I reached the copse without incident, and pulled aside the bracken covering. I smiled. The carrier bag I'd left two nights ago was still here, undisturbed.

I took the bag out, and tipped Andrew Jackson's wrapped body in, covering the grave site over with the bracken and leaves.

I glanced around, and stripped naked.

I stood for a moment, shivering, a smile on my face. I loved the feel of the breeze on my skin, the guilty thrill of potentially being caught out.

As I stood there, naked in the moonlight, the breeze playing over the supple strength of my flanks and shoulders, I felt at home in my body.

I wasn't a woman, when I was naked: I was simply a person with a body full of youth and strength, skin and physical responses.

But I couldn't afford to linger. Bending down, I drew a tracksuit out of the carrier bag, and folded the forensic suit and gloves into it. I tied the bag, and, bringing my arm back as far as it would go, hurled it high and wide. I saw it land in the higher branches of a tree about three feet away. I smiled, and turned away, breaking into a jog.

Just another fitness fanatic, out for an evening's exercise.

## P.C. Tony Raglan
## LB 265

The silence was becoming oppressive. I stood up, staggering a little, wincing. Wyckham glanced up, Feroc turned to look at me.
"I need some fresh air."
"I'll come with you." Wyckham started to get up. I shook my head. "I need some time to myself, Sir. I'll be okay. I'm going to walk down to the woods. That's half an hour each way, give or take. I probably won't be more than an hour once I get there. Couple of hours." I laid a hand on Feroc's shoulder. "Are you going to be alright?"
He nodded. "Yeah. I've got the Inspector here, anyway."
"I'll look after him, Tony."
"Sir." I didn't bother with a jacket, despite the chill in the air – putting on a jacket with my arm in a sling would be too much of a hassle. So far, I hadn't even bothered taking my shoes off. That pleasure could wait until the absolute last minute.
"Tony – take a coat."
I shook my head. "I'll be alright, Fer."
"Tony -"
"It's alright. I'm a big boy – I can take care of myself."
"Well, don't moan at me when you catch pneumonia."
As I stepped out into the cool evening, I wondered if I were unusual, living by the sea but preferring the woods. I couldn't explain why, only that water didn't have anything like the resonance, for me, that trees and stones and the earth had for me.
Feroc was the one for the sea. He never missed an opportunity to go and walk along the beach, to go swimming. Even in a storm, Feroc would be out, heading down to the sea.
I'd seen Feroc swimming in the sea: it was like the currents didn't even exist. He moved as easily in the wilds of the sea as he might in an indoor pool.
Perhaps he had the kind of understanding with and of water as I did with and of earth. Earth: solid, dependable, reliable. Water: fluid, ever-shifting, fickle. Masculine. Feminine. At the end of the

day, there was only ever the binary.

The sun had just started to fall below the horizon when I arrived at the edge of Denes Wood. I started to move towards the pre-set trail, my leg starting to ache a little. The trail was a smooth surface. It would be easier to manage. Somehow, something made me stop, and head into the darkening interior of the wood itself, away from the trail. My leg protested, and my arm was starting to ache, but I felt I had to keep going, as though the decision was being made by someone, or something, else, and I had no option but to follow their instructions.

As I walked, I got an eerie sense that I was treading in someone else's steps. The brush and bracken seemed bent and broken, as though something heavy had recently been dragged across it. The bending was the wrong direction for logging work. Besides, it would surely be easier to pull felled trees along the smooth paths, or at least the cleared logging roads? There was no need to make things harder for yourself, going over wild ground.

The feeling of unease intensified as I walked further into the trees. I was beginning to struggle, pain and unexpected exhaustion bringing my breath through in ragged gasps. I stopped, closing my eyes, shaking my head a little, trying to bring myself round.

When that didn't work, I staggered to a nearby tree stump – a victim of accident or disease, from its raggedness, rather than logging – and slumped down. I forced myself to bring my breathing back under control, closed my eyes, and let my unconscious take over, bringing forward the hidden senses we all have, and use without thinking on a daily basis, to tell me what was going on, and why these woods, so familiar to me normally, so friendly, suddenly felt strange and vaguely threatening.

At first, there was nothing more than the usual static, dots of colour flashing through the blackness behind my eyelids, but, slowly, an image came through, drawings of my subconscious.

A large, powerful black wolf, head held high, framed by a blood red sunset, the framing causing the effect of a heart shape – not anatomically correct, but the way most of us draw hearts when we're being soppy-sweet.

Was the wolf some sort of guardian spirit of the woods? But,if it was, why hadn't I sensed it before? Plus, there hadn't been wolves in Britain for a long time, and I doubted they'd ever lived in the coastal reaches of Lothing.

A messenger from one of my gods? Odin? Loki?

Loki: life born of fire. Loki, the chaotic catalyst. If he were here, it would explain the unease. Of course, if he were here, things were only going to get worse, because Loki never turned up for no reason.

I opened my eyes, blinking slowly – and suddenly came to sudden, awful awareness.

Loki's presence could explain the unease – but it was far more likely that the freshly-dead body, in a nest of rucked-up bracken and torn tarpaulin, was a far more likely suspect.

Whoever had dumped the body here had obviously assumed that Denes Wood didn't play host to the kind of wildlife that would be interested in deceased human. They'd been wrong.

How the hell had I missed the body when I'd sat down? Too caught up in pain, struggling too hard to breathe – I really needed to lose a bit of weight, get a bit fitter. I'd been running on less than empty, energy-wise, for too long. I couldn't just blame the accident on the  bridge for this.

The copper in me stepped smartly forward, shoving the Heathen out of the way with a glare. The copper pulled me to my feet, and led me over to the body.

A man, not young, not old – probably late twenties, early thirties, smartly dressed, although the way he'd put colours together suggested he'd forgotten to call his guide dog through when he'd gone to get dressed.

Then I saw something far more wrong than this guy's fashion sense: the wooden disc, tied to thin black ribbon that was wrapped neatly around the tie, tied off in a small, delicate, feminine bow.

And the runemark, *Fehu,* crudely inked into the centre of the wood.

*Fehu.* Wealth. Success. Prosperity. Good fortune.

But this wasn't a caster. Not a practitioner. There wasn't even the beginnings of respect in the rendering. The runemark was a message, not a rune in and of itself.

I felt suddenly sick. Morgana, living rough and on her wits since that bloody disastrous undercover op all those years ago, would have come into daily, most likely distressing, contact with wealthy, successful people. Smug people. Arrogant people. Perhaps she'd decided to change her victim profile, take out of the world a few more people who'd annoyed, perhaps hurt, her.

A change of symbol for a change of tack? I looked at the body again. This wasn't just a change of tack – this was a change of MO. Morgana spilled blood when she killed – this man had been strangled.

I took my mobile out of my pocket, and called Feroc's phone. I knew he wouldn't answer. I also knew who would.

"Feroc Hanson's phone."

"Guv – it's Tony. Something's happened, out at Denes." I took a breath, hearing Feroc's voice, anxiety rising, in the background. "There's a body. Not natural causes. I think you need to come out here. Is Feroc going to be alright? If you give them a knock at number ninety-two, one of them'll come over and sit with him. We know them...they're...." I paused. "Family."

Wyckham sounded puzzled, but I didn't elaborate. Eventually, I wouldn't need to. He'd work it out.

Wyckham assured me he was on his way. I thanked him, hung up, and, with a deep sigh that spoke far more words than I had, typed a message to a number that was stored under the name "Cass."

THE SEA IS THE LIFEBLOOD OF THE TOWN. AT THE GOING DOWN OF THE SUN, REMEMBER THE SABBATH, AND KEEP IT. ONE STEP BACK.

I sent the message, hoping Morgana understood what I meant: "Meet me by the old fishing trawler, 9pm, Saturday night." Today was Friday. I had to trust firstly that Morgana still had her phone, that it was charged, and that she was sane enough to do as I'd asked.

I hadn't wanted it to be true. Hadn't wanted to believe Morgana had been responsible for killing Claire Jakely. But it was almost impossible that it could be anyone else. Esoteria left on the body was a strange on – there couldn't be any other killers using that MO. Not killing in Lothing, anyway.

This had to be Morgana. It couldn't be anyone else. I'd been wrong, and I'd fought my superiors over it.

I'd gone to bat for a murderer. And my reputation would always be tainted because of it. I was a gay police officer: I couldn't afford to make mistakes. I didn't have the luxury of errors of judgement.

## Inspector Bill Wyckham
## LB 81

"Raglan – get in the car. Feroc refused to have anyone come and stay with him; he's waiting for you, back at yours."

I shouldn't have used his surname. The poor sod looked like a spaniel puppy that'd taken a boot up the backside for no good reason.

I softened my voice.

"I'm not hacked off with you, Tony. You're clearly in shock, and you're not even twenty four hours out of hospital. You're dealing with some pretty intense injuries, and it's getting cold out here." I grinned, trying for light-heartedness. "Plus, you went out without a coat. I'd rather not explain to Feroc that you froze to death. Go on – get in the car. There's a drop of something in the back. Get in the warm, and I'll get you back to your boy as soon as I can, okay?"

He moved like he was in a daze, shaking his head, muttering softly to himself. I watched him go, feeling a growing sense of concern, and took his place by the body.

The first thing I saw was the rune, tied frighteningly neatly around the victims tie.

The same symbol that had been found on Claire Jakely's body. I moaned softly, shaking my head. The chances of two killers using divination symbols as marks – it was almost impossible. And Jessica Kingson had reported a conversation she'd had with a taxi driver – it sounded as though there were concerns being raised about a suspicious-seeming woman, possibly posing as a cab driver.

I took out my phone, and scrolled through to the photograph Jessica had got from the cabbie. I studied the woman in the photo. She didn't look like Morgana Cassidy. The body shape was similar, so was the height. But the hair, the face – those were wrong.

But people changed. Plastic surgery was a thing. If Morgana Cassidy had regained her sanity, but decided that she liked killing?

If she'd found a way to get a lot of cash – and there were several of those avenues open to not unattractive women who ended up on the streets – she might have gone down that route. I couldn't see her in the woman in the photo. I didn't want her to be the killer. But it seemed impossible that she wasn't.

I glanced back at the photo – the businessman approaching the black car looked like the man at my feet. I bent down, picked up a fallen twig and flicked open the man's suit jacket. Pulling the sleeve of my jacket over my hand, I pulled out his wallet: Andrew Jackson.

I replaced the wallet, and took out my mobile phone.

Within twenty minutes, several police vehicles and a forensics van had arrived, crowding the clearing in the woodland, strobing arc lamps through the night darkness. Soon, blue lights and plastic tape had become more dominant in the area than the trees, or at least so it seemed in that moment.

It had begun, then.

An unmarked car pulled up, and Mark Roscoe got out, pulling on a forensics suit and striding over to me, Tam Freud close behind him.

"Bill"

"Mark"

"Tam"

"Sir."

"Alright if I leave this to you, Mark?"

"I'm not a hundred percent on why you're here to begin with?"

"Tony Raglan found the body."

"Raglan? What was he doing out here?"

"He needed a walk – cabin fever. I did offer to go with him, but he needed his own company. He's in the back of my motor now. I want to get him home – he looks done in."

"Alright – the interview can wait until the morning – this fella's not going anywhere. We know who he is yet?"

I nodded. "I had a look in his wallet. Andrew Jackson." I showed Mark Roscoe the photo on my phone. "One of my PCs, Jessica

Kingson, spoke to a taxi driver who had some concerns about another driver – the woman in the photograph. This is the same man, I'm pretty sure."

"And the woman is probably Morgana Cassidy. I had a look at her file, Bill – the build, the height, it's spot on."

"But not the rest."

"Plastic surgery is a thing, Bill. And hair dye."

I shook my head. "I won't go for it, Mark."

"Keep an open mind, eh, Bill?"

"I don't like the idea of open minds – brains tend to fall out."

"Bill... I know you're not going to like it if, as is entirely likely, we get Morgana Cassidy for this, but, if – when – we do, you're going to need to deal with it. Okay?"

"If Morgana Cassidy is responsible for this, I'll be the first to deal with it, fully and appropriately. Thank you for your concern, though."

## DI Mark Roscoe

None of us wanted to admit what was almost certain: Morgana Cassidy had regained her sanity, certainly enough to alter her appearance, but had not lost her lust for murder.

But Bill Wyckham was right – something was off about this. I'd checked the files: there'd been no murders with her signature for about two years. That wasn't a long time when it came to murderers, but it was worth bearing in mind. Of course, it could mean that she'd taken that time to plan her next course of action, decide on her new victim profile.

It could also, as Bill Wyckham would protest, mean that this wasn't her.

I had to agree with him – the woman in the photograph might share Morgana Cassidy's height and build, but then so do a good many women. But then, women didn't tend to be murderers. Women didn't kill, especially not in public ways. Not like this.

Whatever Bill Wyckham might think, I didn't want this to be down to Morgana Cassidy. She was still, just about, family.

But not if these two killings were down to her. The others could have been squared away – wheel out the psych squad, get reports talking about post-traumatic stress, have long, rambling discussions about difficult situations, extreme stress, emotional vulnerability, insufficient supervision, questionable managerial decisions, opportunities missed... But these murders were different. They were clearly pre-meditated. There wasn't any way they could be written off.

Some small part off me was calmly and quietly telling me that we were going to miss a dangerous killer by focusing on Morgana Cassidy for these deaths. The rest of me was screaming that Morgana was going to swing for these killings, that the full force of the law should be going after that bitch like the Hounds of Hell.

You might have noticed that coppers don't like being lied to. Or betrayed.

"Right – what've we got?"

Tam Freud straightened up. "Andrew Jackson. Thirty one. There's a season rail ticket to London, and a pass code for … Chancery, Delauney, De'ath. Whoever they are when they're at home."

I recognised the name from a trade show I'd been discreetly asked by the organisers – and not so discreetly ordered by my Guv'nor – to police, quietly and politely.

"They're an investment firm in the City." Tam raised an eyebrow. "I'm guessing we're not talking about Norwich."

"No. And we're not talking about the East End, either. Very posh, very exclusive."

"Coppers not welcome?"

"Senior managers, maybe. People with very good salaries, and even better pensions."

"Right.  So... mobile phone, latest bit of kit...." Tam turned to the SOCO officer who was bagging items and property. "Make sure that wooden disc is prioritised. It links this to another murder."

The SOCO nodded. I stepped forward, something having  caught my eye. I pointed to the marks around the victim's neck. "What would have caused marks like that? I've not seen them before on a strangulation case."

The SOCO crouched beside the body, peering at the marks from several angles. She motioned to an assistant to take some photographs.  She fingered the marks, head on one side, and stood up. "I can't be a hundred percent, but it looks very much like small, hard, round beads. Possibly pearls."

"*Pearls?*"

"Yes. Possibly a pearl necklace, although it would have had to have been custom strung. A regular string would have snapped."

I was incredulous. "Someone strangled this guy with a *pearl necklace?*"

"A necklace, certainly. A necklace comprised of round beads. Hard, round beads. My guess? You're looking for a very strong, or very angry, woman." She smiled. "Or a man who is completely comfortable with his masculinity, and doesn't have any issues with wearing nice jewellery."

### D.C. Tam Freud

I saw the look on the DI's face when the SOCO explained what had, in all probability, caused Andrew Jackson's death. When she told him he was most likely looking for a woman. An angry, strong woman.

Like just about everyone at Lothing, I'd heard about Morgana Cassidy, the copper who'd flipped out and run to the dark side, leaving a trail of blood and bodies in her wake. I'd joined Lothing as a uniformed PC about a year after everything had gone down.

I suppressed a wholly inappropriate hope that these killings were down to Morgana Cassidy – I had a strange desire to meet her. Awful as it sounded, I felt that I'd get on well with her.

What bothered me about everything to do with Morgana Cassidy was that people who were crazy – genuinely crazy – often weren't a danger to others. To themselves, yes, but not usually to other people, to strangers. I could see her killing the men who'd been in the house with her, in a moment of extreme stress, of psychosis, maybe, but it was a stretch to think of someone completely unhinged pursuing an agenda of murder. And certainly not of being aware enough to leave a very obvious, very deliberate mark at the scenes.

If Morgana Cassidy was suffering from some kind of reactive mental illness, some kind of stress-induced psychosis, which, in her case, had resulted in her becoming unusually dangerous to others, then that was interesting, to me at least, from a psychological standpoint.

If she were not mentally unstable, however, I wanted to meet her as one woman admiring the sheer ruthlessness of another, who was able to kill seemingly without any kind of emotional kickback, and without any anxiety around being caught. And a woman who had killed, several times, yet managed to stay several steps ahead of the law.

In short, I wanted to know whether Morgana Cassidy was mad, or bad.

## P.C. Feroc Hanson
## LB 599

When Tony came in, Wyckham almost leading him, as though he were some kind of stray puppy, he looked like he'd aged ten years. He crossed the room to his usual armchair as though he were sleepwalking, not even looking up when the parrot screeched his name. Idaho clearly sensed that something was up: instead of keeping up the screeching, as he normally would, he settled into a low, mournful muttering, repeating Tony's name over and over again.

"Tony? What's happened? The Inspector wouldn't tell me anything." In the silence of Tony's refusal to respond, I turned to Wyckham. "Sir?"

Wyckham sighed. "Tony found a body, in Denes Wood. A murder. With the same runemark that was found on Claire Jakely's body."

"Oh, Tony – are you alright? How bad was it? Tony, are you okay?"

"He'd been strangled." It came out as a hoarse whisper. Tony still didn't look up. "It wasn't...I've seen worse. You will, too."

Strangled. I glanced at Wyckham. "Like Claire Jakely?" He nodded. "Yes."

"So it's the same killer?"

"Almost certainly."

Tony looked up. "But not Morgana." He sounded less convinced than he had previously, though, as though he were beginning to doubt his one-time friend's innocence. That, more than anything else, broke my heart. I couldn't imagine how much it must have cost Tony, to even consider the possibility that he'd been wrong, that he'd been protecting a copper who'd gone rogue.

"Anything decent on telly?" I recognised the change of tone – Tony was trying to avoid thinking the obvious thoughts about the latest killing, Claire Jakely's murder, and Morgana Cassidy.

"There's something about automation – robots taking over everyone's jobs."

"Well, that sounds soul-destroyingly depressing."

"You reckon coppers could be replaced with robots, then?"

"Makes sense, doesn't it? It'd be easy enough to programme them to recognise various crimes, and programme them to respond with 'reasonable force' – no complaints, no lawsuits, no leave, no salary. No expense, and robots don't need refs, or sleep. No need for mobile units, either."

"Thing is, though, if robots ever got to that point, wouldn't there be a case to suggest they were entitled to rights?"

"Rights are payment for the fulfilment of responsibilities, Feroc. You can hardly be said to be fulfilling responsibilities if you're simply doing what you're programmed to do, can you?"

"So you think that only people who fulfil responsibilities have rights?" Wyckham sounded genuinely interested.

"Yes. It's why you get your rights revoked when you're in prison, or committed to a psyche unit, isn't it?"

"What about children or old people then?"

"Well, kids are going to be fulfilling responsibilities, at some point, and old people already have."

"It's an interesting premise."

Tony, seeming somewhat more animated, turned to me. "So, you reckon robots could take over your writing, Fer?"

I laughed. "One day. But not in my lifetime. I hope."

Tony nodded. "You're working again, aren't you? I saw your nice, shiny new notebook when I was looking for my chequebook, the day before... well, before we first came across the fallout from Claire Jakely's murder."

"Your chequebook's in the bureau in the hall. Where we keep things relating to banking?" I was trying not to laugh.

"I didn't see it."

"Want me to go and look?" Wyckham looked at me.

"Yeah, why not? Maybe I'm mis-remembering. Middle drawer. Key's in the inside pocket of the grey blazer on the coat rack."

"Okay."

Wyckham headed out. Less than five minutes later, he was back.

"Two chequebooks – one in the name of Feroc Hanson, one in the name of Tony Raglan. Right on top of the drawer."

Tony grinned sheepishly. "Like I said, I didn't see them."
Wyckham gave a mock-serious frown. "When did you last have
an eye test, Raglan?"
"And anyway, " I added, "you shouldn't use 'nice' – it's a
meaningless word that tells no one anything."
Wyckham looked confused. "'Again?' What does he mean
'again?'"
I blushed. "I, ah..."
"He's written a book – you can get it off Amazon. *New Blue.*"
"Sounds worrying." Wyckham turned to me, jerking his head in
Tony's direction. "He in it?"
"Yeah – but not in that way."
His eyes widened. "Am *I* in it?"
I laughed. "You'll have to buy it and find out, won't you, Guv?"
"What, and finance your immoral lifestyle?"
"I thought the taxpayer was already doing that."

## RAGNAROK

I hadn't planned on a police officer finding Andrew Jackson. He was supposed to have been found by a clueless member of the public, an eventuality which would have ensured a messy reporting, and a fair lead time before anyone sussed what was going on. Ideally, the rune was supposed to have been taken, either torn off by a dog, or taken by the dozy finder, who didn't realise it was important and wanted a keepsake of their first actual, proper, murdered body.

It wasn't supposed to happen so quickly. I wasn't ready.

I paced around my hotel room, thinking furiously, Should I go ahead, and start planning another murder? Should I leave it for now? If so, how long was I going to be out of the game for? I hadn't yet identified a third victim – it would be easy enough to hold off.

I could back off – but every instinct, my whole heart and soul, rebelled against the idea. I was a professional. I'd started a strong, beautiful series, and I needed to see it through.

I sat down at the cheap wooden desk, and opened up my laptop. Time to start browsing, see who some likely players in the immoral earnings, undeservedly wealthy category of this world were.

The story was underway – and it wanted to be told.

## Inspector Bill Wyckham
## LB 81

I went into work the following morning with a lighter heart than I'd had for a while.

 Feroc's sister had arrived just before eight, about fifteen minutes before I left, looking harassed

"Where the hell is this place? Beirut? I couldn't find Waitrose, and M&S didn't have any jumbo cous cous, or quinoa.  There are probably refugee camps that are better stocked."

She'd glanced between me and Tony. "So, which one of you is Tony?"

"Hi. You must be Maevynne." Tony's voice had been his usual laconic drawl. She'd scowled at him.

"Well, I can see why a lack of complex carbohydrates and pulse-based nutrition wouldn't be a problem to *you.*"

Tony had raised an eyebrow. "Nice to finally meet you in person, too."

Maevynne had stropped through to the kitchen, and slammed down the shopping bags she'd arrived with. "Oh, thank god – you actually do have the means to procure vegetables out here."

"Maevynne – stop being a bitch, yeah?"

"I'm not 'being a bitch', Feroc – I'm worried about you. I mean, you're in a *wheelchair* for crying out loud! You're never going to get properly better eating junk, are you?"

Feroc had laughed, and turned to Tony. "I don't know...he seems strong enough on it."

I'd laughed – then beat a hasty retreat before the Magnificent Maevynne, who may or may not have been a reincarnation of Boudicca, decided to lash out at me, too.

 "Sir?"

"Leah – what can I do for you?"

"I ran the basics on last night's victim – name and address all check out, Andrew Jackson, thirty-one, late of twelve, The Street, Teighdene, no previous police contact, no criminal record. No associates known to us."

Just like Claire Jakely. A seemingly snow-white citizen who'd got himself killed.

Tony Raglan had a theory that nobody got killed for no reason. If you got yourself murdered, according to Tony Raglan, you'd somehow, somewhere along the line, done something to someone who'd decided your death was the only appropriate response to the offence.

I wondered what Claire Jakely and Andrew Jackson had done, other than possibly having surnames that began with the tenth letter of the alphabet.

Maybe that was the pattern. Maybe our killer didn't like people whose surnames started with the letter J. Or that had a K in them.

But something about Claire Jakely was nagging at me. Like, what was she doing at thirty-eight Haresfoot Way, for a start.

"Right, Leah – we were pretty much expecting that, but thanks anyway."

"Sir."

I went into my office, shut the door, and put the kettle on. Booting up the computer, I sat down, hesitating between two possibly courses of action.

As the kettle reached its climax, I made my decision – but I'd make my coffee first.

Two minutes later, I was typing Claire Jakely's name into Google. The first result that came up was a website called 'Woman's Will.' I took a gulp of coffee, and clicked through to the site.

WOMAN'S WILL – LIFESTYLE ADVICE, GUIDANCE, AND DEVELOPMENT FOR THE PROFESSIONAL WOMAN.

I scanned through the site. So far, so much as the file had reported. But something still nagged. I clicked on to the LINKS page. Pages for interior design, gyms, fashion brands, events.

And, at the bottom of the list, not rendered as a link, a series of letters and numbers: DMBS 999 776676

The website designer's tag? I clicked back to Google, and typed the letters and numbers into the search bar.

CLAIRE CONTROL – DOMINATION FOR THE
DISCERNINGLY OBEDIENT.

I clicked the page header, already knowing what I was likely to
find.
 Claire Jakely had been a professional dominatrix.
I picked up the phone on my desk, and dialled three numbers, an
internal extension code.
"Mark? It's Bill Wyckham. I've got something here I need you to
look at. Don't bring anyone with you unless you can trust them
fifteen-thousand percent not to freak out, blab, or otherwise cause
a problem."
People had a strange habit of confessing to murders they hadn't
committed, which meant there was always something, some key
fact, that the police kept back. Something that only the real killer
was likely to know.  I had a feeling that Claire Jakely's BDSM
connections were that fact – and were the reason Tony Raglan
believed always existed for someone being murdered.

 Ten minutes later, Mark Roscoe sat back, shaking his head, and
looked at me.
"I'd like to bring Tam Freud in on this. She's apparently got a mate
– not in the Job – who's into this sort of thing. She might be able
to talk to her, get a bit of insight. Maybe the woman knows Claire
Jakely."
I nodded. "Do it. Discreetly."
Roscoe took out a mobile phone, and tapped keys. "Tam? Drop by
Bill Wyckham's office, will you? On the QT, please."

### Maevynne Hanson

"Waitrose don't deliver here!"

Feroc tried not to laugh. Tony – I still couldn't quite get my head around calling him Feroc's "partner", and I didn't think I'd ever get used to the idea of him as "my brother-in-law" - wasn't quite as successful.

 I wasn't homophobic, but Feroc was so attractive, so bright, so competent – he deserved something better, as far as I could see.

"I don't see what's so funny."

"Look, Maevynne – this isn't Cambridge.  But, as you've seen, we do have vegetables around here."

"But apparently not Waitrose."

I was aware that I was being petulant, but I somehow couldn't manage to stop.

"No. Not Waitrose. But there is a health food shop. Up on the High Street. Origami."

Feroc laughed – it had been so long since I'd heard my brother's laugh. It sounded like waves falling on shattered glass. That description doesn't sound as beautiful as Feroc's laugh was. He turned to Tony. "Orega*no*, Tone. It's named after a herb, not Japanese paper folding."

"Oregano, Origami – same difference. It probably sells cous cous, and... whatever the other thing was."

"Keen-waaahhh." I sounded it out slowly, deliberately, as though I were talking to a child.

 This wasn't lost on Tony Raglan.

"I thought that was a country in Africa?  Look, Maevynne, I'm not an idiot. I'm not stupid. So I haven't heard of something posh nobs eat.  That doesn't make me scum."

I glared. "Feroc is what you call a 'posh nob', in case you weren't aware."

"Not any more. And I only ever was one through an accident of birth. I never agreed with a lot of Mum's attitudes, certainly. Dad wasn't too bad.  Look, Maev, I know this is...difficult for you, bur I'm happy with Tony. I'm happy as a copper."

"You're in a *wheelchair!* How can you be happy about being a police officer, when it was being a police officer that put you there?"

The look Feroc gave me made me feel about five years old. "It's only temporary. A couple of weeks. There are some people, Maev, who are in wheelchairs for life. Children. People who are in wheelchairs because someone got drunk, and then got into a car. People who are in wheelchairs because doctors screwed up. People who are in wheelchairs because of a stupid, daft, preventable accident. Yes, I'm going to have scars – my first scars. Tony's covered in them. They're a map, of the places we've been, a photo album of the things we've seen. They're tattoos. And, like tattoos, they tell stories. I'll never be ashamed of my stories, Maev. I'll never regret them. And I will never, ever, regret being what I am, and loving the man I love."

I sighed. "I didn't mean... Feroc, you have to understand, what you are, what you do, doesn't just affect you. I'd always imagined meeting some woman who was your fiancée, a woman who'd become your wife. I imagined us having girly chats, going shopping together -"

"I'm sure Tony could cope with a girly shopping spree in Norwich, couldn't you, Tone?"

"Yeah – I've always wanted to try on those little denim shorts they do. Maybe with a pair of high heels – I've seen some black leather ones with spikes on that look quite cool. They have matching handbags, I think."

I couldn't help it – I started laughing. Tony got up, and laid his hand on my shoulder.

"That's a good start, Maevynne. I know you've dealt with a lot of disappointments over Feroc's sexuality, and there're probably going to be many more – I know I'm not what most women imagine when they think of their brothers' life partners . And I'm sorry that he's got injured, in part because of me, in part because of the Job, in part because of a number of other people and factors that no one could have controlled or predicted. But don't start out hating me, yeah? We've got the rest of our lives for you to become the sister-in-law from hell."

I took a deep breath, and closed my eyes. When I opened them, I didn't see the man who'd stolen my brother's future. I didn't see an overweight slob who'd settled for a less than stellar career performance.

Instead, I saw a quiet, gentle, wounded man with a lifetime of sorrow in his eyes. I saw a man who, being so much older than Feroc, had presumably had to surrender far more than Feroc to be who and what he was.

I held out my hand. Tony Raglan took it in his good hand, the one which wasn't dangling from a sling. I smiled. "I'm sorry. I..."

"You're worried about Feroc. About your brother. I understand."

"Yes. I... We got off on the wrong foot. I was stressed, terrified about what I was going to find when I turned up here, and I took it out on you. That was unfair."

"Well, let's see if we can get on a better foot – shall I walk you up to the green-coloured shop, into which I have never set foot, which is either named after a herb, or Japanese paper folding, and see if you can find this foodstuff that sounds like a country?"

I studied his face. "Are you sure you're well enough?"

Tony laughed. "It's five minutes up the road. I don't think I'll have a heart attack or a diabetes flare in that time."

"Are you -"

"Diabetic? No. I don't have high blood pressure, either. Give me a minute to make sure Feroc's sorted, and I'll be with you."

As Tony Raglan took hold of Feroc's wheelchair, spinning him round to face the door into the hallway, I got to my feet. "Tony?" He turned.

"Thank you."

"No worries. You never know – I might even like this country-named food of yours."

### D.C. Tam Freud

I looked up from Claire Jakely's website, wondering how we could have missed it the first time round, why no one had thought that that alphanumeric string looked...out of place.

But then, it *was* worked into a tribal design – it could easily have been dismissed as the site designer's logo. Such people were known to have some rather strange ideas of what made good business branding.

I turned to my DI, first. "Yes, Guv. This is the kind of thing Debbie's into."

"How likely is it she'd have known Claire Jakely?"

"Known of her, known her name, known her to speak to? Very likely – it's a small community, especially in Lothing. Known her personally? Much less so – Debbie just does this for fun. Claire Jakely was a pro, from the looks of this."

"Fun?" Roscoe shook his head. "I don't even see how it can be legal, never mind fun."

"Some of it isn't. Legal, I mean." I turned to Inspector Wyckham. "Congrats on finding this, Sir – the rest of us missed it."

"I nearly did – I assumed, at first, it was just the site designer's signature. I don't know what made me Google it – idle curiosity, probably. And a sense that there had to be something wrong about Claire Jakely. People don't get murdered for no reason."

I smiled, recognising the theory. "Tony Raglan? How's he doing? And Feroc?"

"They're fine – or they were. Feroc's sister arrived shortly before I left for work this morning – she seems like a real piece of work."

I laughed. "Good. Tony Raglan needs to be challenged."

The uniform Inspector grinned. "That he does – it's why I like ensuring that your paths intersect every so often."

"I'm not challenging, Sir."

"That's not what Tony Raglan would say."

The DI interrupted. "How soon can you talk to this Debbie woman?"

"She doesn't work weekends, Guv – I can give her a call just now?"

He nodded. "Do it. From here, though. I don't want this getting out, not even to other coppers in the nick."

I understood – this was a key point about Claire Jakely's life, something that, in all probability, was known specifically to her killer. We needed to keep the media away from it, so we had half a chance of nailing the right person.

Was that person Morgana Cassidy? No one had said anything further about her, so I wondered if this new information cast her role in proceedings into doubt.

I took out my mobile, and swiped through to Debbie's number. I waited several rings, and was about to hang up when she finally answered.

"Hey! Tam! Sorry, I was in the shower. How're you doing?"

"Good. You?"

"Yeah, you know – keeping on keeping on."

"Look, Debs, this is work – would it be okay if I popped round later? I need to run some stuff by you, and I need to have your word you won't talk to anyone else about it."

"All sounds very thrilling. And of course – if someone asks me to keep something quiet, I tend to assume there's a damn good reason for *needing* it kept quiet. Don't worry, Tam – you tell me, and it'll be like you told a tombstone. Come round in about half an hour – I should be decent, and decently caffeinated, by then."

"Okay. Thanks, Debs. See you in about half an hour." I ended the call, and glanced at Roscoe and Wyckham. "She's onside with keeping it under wraps."

Roscoe nodded, a single inclining of his head. "Good. Spend as long as you need with her – treat it as a catch-up session, if you like. It's the weekend, and, if as is looking somewhat likely, we have a serial killer strolling around, this may be the last point at which things are not completely manic. If I need you, I'll call you, but let me know soon as if she does know anything about Claire Jakely. And you may as well ask about Andrew Jackson, while you're there. Maybe that's the link, the BDSM stuff."

Inspector Wyckham frowned. "But that's nothing to do with the

meaning of the rune. *Fehu*'s related to wealth, prosperity."
Roscoe shrugged. "If Andrew Jackson turns out to have been ' involved in BDSM, Bill, then the rune is probably either a random quirk, something our perp happens to like – or I've been right all along, and it's Morgana Cassidy, trying to get a message to Tony Raglan."
"I'm not buying that, Mark."
I stood up. "Well, I'll see what Debbie has to say about both of them. You may be right, Sir – this may have nothing to do with BDSM, beyond Claire Jakely's involvement."
The uniformed Inspector sighed, and turned to his computer. "I'll do the obvious, and run a Google search on Jackson just now." He tapped at the keyboard, clicked, and waited. After a few minutes' scrolling and clicking, he shook his head. "If there is something, it's not obvious – just a lot of stuff about the firm he worked for, a blog he ran on affordable – and I use that word loosely, although I think he thought he was being serious – investments. Nothing much else. His LinkedIn profile is so-so, his Facebook profile is wholly inoffensive."
I grinned. "Maybe he was killed for being boring."
"Maybe so. I haven't come across that as a motive, yet, but I know far better than to say it *can't* be a motive. Someone will kill someone for being boring, one day. People kill people for not liking the same music they do, for pity's sake."
"Do they, or is that just an urban myth?" The DI looked edgy, the way he always did when he was on the scent of something. I'd worked with him long enough to know when he was straining at the leash, and he was wild with the chase right now. I almost felt sorry for our perp, when they were eventually found: Detective Inspector Roscoe was going to give them hell.
"I'll call as soon as I have a definite answer, Guv." I was on my feet, picking up my handbag. The Guv'nor nodded.
"Catch you later, Tam. Take it easy."
"Guv." As the door closed behind me, I had a sense of absolute certainty, even though I'd never known her, that these murders were not down to Morgana Cassidy. There was no evidence Claire

162

Jakely got involved with anyone other than consenting adults, and no evidence that Morgana Cassidy went after anyone who wasn't in some way involved in violating consent.

As I crossed the yard to my car, it struck me that there was no evidence of Morgana Cassidy being involved in any kind of murder, that I'd heard. Maybe I just wasn't being told things, or maybe things weren't there to tell.

I arrived at Debbie's thirty-three minutes after I'd called her. She answered almost as soon as I knocked. We hugged, reassured each other that it was good to see each other again, and I stepped across her threshold, and into a house I always envied.

Debbie Barnes was one of those people who could pull a flawless look together with next to no money, and no formal background in interior design. Her current scheme was urban-focused: her hallway featured a red telephone box landline phone, which sat on an industrial filing cabinet, and a series of meat hooks serving as a coat rack on the opposite wall. The wallpaper was stylised graffiti, and instead of carpet there was black rubber matting designed to look and feel like tarmac.

The living room featured a children's playroom carpet, with the road network of a small pretend town, buildings and parks dotted around. The coffee table appeared to have been fashioned from an old steel dustbin, lidless and upturned, and the shelves, filled with books, were warehouse racking. A desktop PC sat on top of a stainless steel work bench, a hairdressing salon stool in front of it.

The sofa, and its matching armchair, were black leather. The walls were plain white, each with a large, seemingly hand-painted road sign taking up a vast swathe of the centre.

From the kitchen, I could smell brewing coffee and baking. "How the hell can you be so bloody good at *everything*?" I laughed, looking round. "This is amazing."

"You like it? I've redone the garden, too – come through and look. The brownies should be done by now. We can have them with coffee - they've got cranberries and cashew nuts in them."

I shook my head. "They're going to make it illegal to be multitalented. Any day now."

Debbie grinned. "Oh well – prison might be a good source of inspiration. Come through. Don't worry about your shoes."

I followed her back through the hall, into a kitchen that was all steel and copper, thick wooden butchers' slabs on each counter top. Out of the window, I saw the garden – and gasped.

The last time I'd been here, Debbie had been scratching her head over what to do with the overgrown wildness beyond her back door. Now, it had been gravelled over, and more steel dustbins stood, upright this time, sprouting heads of sprawling wildflowers. In the centre, old tires of various styles and sizes formed a network of water features. Piles of brick rubble, and artfully placed broken piping completed the effect, which was surrounded and signed off by a wire mesh fence, placed up against the unpainted, unvarnished wooden version that Debbie's neighbours clearly wouldn't have taken kindly to having removed.

"Debs, this is amazing."

"Thanks," she smiled, pouring coffee. "I'm thinking of looking into whether I can get an adult-sized swing set for the far corner over there. What do you think?"

I took a proffered mug of coffee. "I think you're a genius."

"Not quite, but I try. Brownie?"

"Please. And I'm serious, Debs – you should go into doing this as a job."

"I've thought about it," she admitted, pulling out the rack of brownies, and placing one on a plate. "Careful – they're still hot."

"Leave it with the others to cool, then. I've been told to take as long as I need."

"That important, eh? You'd better bring your coffee through, and tell me what it's all about."


"Yes, I know – knew – Claire Jakely. Not well, but Dominant women tend to stick close in the lifestyle. Even if we're not involved with each other, we keep tabs on each other. It's more a protection thing than anything else – you need to know who's playing what with whom, so if a predator turns up, you can warn people who are at risk of getting hurt."

"That makes sense. What did you think of her?"

"Claire?" Debbie pulled a face. "She was a bit up herself, but then some people can be. Especially the pros – they think they're automatically better than us "Weekend Whip Hands", as they like to call us."

"Did she make any enemies?"

"Probably, but not the kind who would kill her. Her reputation, maybe, if they could, but not her, herself."

"Any bad clients?"

Debbie laughed. "The kind of people who go to pro Dommes are usually men, yes, and I get that men are more likely to kill, but not these men. If they got angry with Claire, or a woman like her, they'd take great delight in 'fessing up, and begging to be punished for their 'improper thoughts.' Subs don't kill – they get angry in order to be punished, if they're Brats, but they don't kill."

"I'll have to come out with you more often – all these different terms sound fascinating. What about the men in the lifestyle? Do you know them?"

"Some. Not as well as I know the other women, though. Who're you thinking of?"

I showed her the photo we had, pre-death, of Andrew Jackson, since his name was quite common, and there was every chance he'd been using an alias, if he had been in the lifestyle. Debbie studied the photo, and shook her head. "No. I think I'd remember someone like him – if he were in the lifestyle, he'd definitely be a Dominant, and the kind that made a point of getting himself noticed."

"There are other kinds?"

"Oh, yeah." She nodded enthusiastically. "A guy I've double-dommed with before, someone I only know as Darke Wolfe – with an E at the end of both Darke and Wolfe – is the most quiet, unassuming guy you could meet who's still not a sub." She paused. "I mean, he's not unassuming to look at – very Mr. Tall Dark and Terrifying – and he's certainly not unassuming when he plays – but in general, personality-wise, he's not interested whether you notice him or not. He's happy if you're not into playing with him, he doesn't care if you know his name or his reputation. That's *very* unusual in a guy. Mind you, he's not a Dom."

"But you just said he's not a sub."

"He's not." She smiled, as though recalling a particularly pleasant memory. "Darke Wolfe is a Sadist. And a very, very good one."

"A Sadist? And you can say that like it's a *good* thing?" The copper in me had her hackles up.

"It is, the way Darke Wolfe does it – with him, it's about mutual pleasure. He's not out to make anyone suffer. He wants to help them transcend whatever's brought them to him. He wants to make them better people, stronger people. I mean, yes, he breaks people, he enjoys breaking people – but only so he can put them back together again."

I shivered. "I can't imagine many people want to be broken."

"Not by a man, no. He loses out a lot to the female Sadists – women like Claire Jakely. But that doesn't bother him. I asked him, once, if it did – he just shrugged, and said that he'd rather people knew what they wanted than played with him, and bitched because he *wasn't* what they wanted. Like I say, he's all about consent, and mutual enjoyment."

"I still don't think Sadism has any place being even halfway legitimate."

Debbie gave me a serious look. "Come out with me next Saturday. There's a Munch – it's a low key affair, there is some play, but it's usually just among the regulars. There's food, drink, good conversation. Darke Wolfe has been asked to do a demonstration, and talk a bit about how he sees Sadism, and his role as a Sadist. I'll introduce you."

"Okay – but only if I get more of these amazing brownies as a reward for not arresting this guy on sight."

Debbie broke into a grin. "Trust me, after five minutes with him, you won't want to even consider arresting him."

## DI Mark Roscoe

I shut down my phone, and looked over at Bill Wyckham.
"It seems Andrew Jackson wasn't involved in the BDSM
community, at least not locally, and Tam's mate hadn't seen him at
any of the occasional events she attends in London. So... we're
back to Morgana Cassidy."

"Are we, though?" He regarded me, a pained, concerned
expression on his face. "We've got a photograph of a woman who
looks not very much like her, except in very vague, very general
terms, with the dead man earlier that day. We've got an MO that's
nothing like Morgana Cassidy's, victims who don't match her
profile. And, finally, we've actually got nothing more than strong
suspicion and circumstantial evidence that Morgana Cassidy ever
killed anyone anyway."

I blinked, stunned. "You what?"

"You've read the file, Mark. No forensics was ever found at any of
the crime scenes. We believe the murders we've tagged as hers
were committed by her because of her shoulder number being left
at the crime scene. But that's circumstantial, it's not conclusive."

"I'd say it's pretty damn close!"

"But would the CPS? I can see a smart defence lawyer arguing
that, as Morgana Cassidy and Tony Raglan were close, he could
have committed the murders, and set it up to look as though
Morgana were responsible, knowing full well we'd never find
her."

"How would he know that? Unless -"

Bill Wyckham nodded. "Unless he was still in contact with her.
Which I believe he is."

My mouth was dry. I shook my head. "You don't think -?"

"No. I don't. He was on duty, here in Lothing, when at least two of
the murders were committed. But it's a possible argument – in
theory, anyone who knew Morgana's history and shoulder number
could have committed those murders. Or the '741' on the tarot
cards might relate to something else entirely.

I shook my head again, slowly. "You really are a good copper, aren't you, Bill?"

He grinned. "Well, they don't hand stripes out with special packs of Carlsberg Export, that's for sure." He paused. "Speaking of which, there's a Sergeant's board coming up next year. I just had the memo through."

"So did I."

"You going to put Freud forward?"

"Yes. Definitely. She's keen for it. What about you? Any of yours you think are ready?"

"Tony Raglan, but he won't go for it – God knows why. He'd make a good Sergeant. Feroc Hanson's got to be my choice. Although, if he does go for it, and he gets it – which I can't see how he won't – there's the small question of how Tony's going to react to him almost certainly moving on."

I shook my head. "Raglan's sound. He wouldn't stand in Feroc's way."

Bill Wyckham smiled. "You know, the strange thing is, Feroc actually said the exact same thing to Tony Raglan, the day he got shot, when we were all back at the nick – 'when the time comes, Tony, I won't stand in your way.' It sounded odd, even then, and I still can't quite work out what he meant."

I frowned. "You're right. It doesn't make sense. Unless Feroc knows more about Tony's ambitions than we do?"

He shook his head. "Tony Raglan's sole ambition, now, is to be a good beat copper. He's said as much. But Feroc must know something about him. There must be something that he knows he's going to have to stand aside for, so that Tony can get something he's long been after. But I'm damned if I know what it is."

There was a knock at the door that had us both on our feet. "Come."

A young female PC came in – I recognised her from the Claire Jakely scene, Leah Black. Wyckham nodded in greeting.

"Leah – what is it?"

"Andrew Jackson, Sir – I thought you'd like to know: he was in to child porn. We found an external hard drive, hidden at the back of his wardrobe. It's full of the stuff. There are magazines, too."

Wyckham groaned, and I felt his frustration. This was probably the motive for Andrew Jackson's murder, but it was going to make finding his killer that bit more difficult – any number of people could have stumbled on his guilty secret, and all of them wouldn't have hesitated to kill him over it, either to try and get his material for themselves, in the case of other nonces, or in outrage, in the case of just about everyone else.

"Has it been bagged and tagged?"

"Yes, Sir. We're bringing it in now."

"Get it straight up to CID." Wyckham turned to me. "You'd best be off, Detective Inspector – seems like you're going to be kept busy."

I nodded, pushing back my chair and getting to my feet in one smooth movement. "In the worst way possible."

## Morgana

I didn't have any credit on my mobile, but I did have a train pass, thanks to my support worker.

 Helen had helped me a lot, since I'd come to the shelter about two years ago, after I'd read about Tony Raglan getting shot, in a newspaper someone had just thrown away.  I always took newspapers out of bins – you never knew when you might see something interesting, or important. When there might be a job or something listed, a chance for you to try and turn your life around.

 I'd slowly been coming back to myself, before that day, leaving longer and longer periods of time before I felt I *had* to go and kill someone, some scumbag who'd hurt women, or children, or both. I saw enough of them, every day. I had plenty of choice.  But, slowly, I'd been losing the taste for it, feeling that it wasn't solving anything.

And then I'd read about Tony being shot, and I'd been so upset, so terrified that he might die, and I'd never be able to say goodbye. And then I'd realised that, whatever the men I killed had done, they had people who were heartbroken by their deaths. People who'd wanted the chance to say goodbye.

 I knew I wouldn't be able to stay on the streets and not kill, so I'd walked until I'd found the hostel I'd read about in the paper a few weeks before. I was pleased I'd remembered it – not the name, but the fact that it had a rainbow-coloured flower in its emblem.  I just looked for the flower, and eventually found it.

 I don't think they'd been expecting people to just turn up, but they'd found me a room, a proper room, where it was just me, and there was a cupboard for my things, and a desk, and a bathroom that was just mine, and I'd settled down to living at what I learned was called Bright Growth House – or, as some of the women who lived here called it, "Be Good, Hen" - that was after something one of the support workers always said. She was from Yorkshire, or up North somewhere, and was always calling people 'Hen'. I'd been given six weeks to settle in, to 'find my feet, make some friends', as the lady in charge, Bridget, had termed it, and then I'd met Helen, and we'd been meeting twice a week, every week, except for when she was on holiday, ever since, talking about everything – I didn't have to talk about my feelings if I didn't want to,or if I wasn't really having any, and she was quite happy for me not to talk at all, but just to draw, or sit and read, or even just stare out of the window.

In the past few months, Helen had taken me shopping, taken me to get my hair cut, taken me to the dentist and the opticians. We had a doctor at the hostel – the 'home', as we were supposed to call it, Dr. Keenan, and she was very good, and kind. Kindness is important. It's what I'd liked about Tony Raglan: he'd always been kind.

I read his text again, working out what time he meant. Nine o'clock tonight. I wasn't supposed to be out that late, but I'd spoken to Bridget, and told her a friend needed help, and she'd booked me a bed – not a proper room, just a bed in a dormitory, but it was all women – at a hostel in Lothing.

"Call me when you get to Lothing, go and have something to eat, and something to drink, then go and meet your friend. The hostel will call here once you've arrived there – go straight there from meeting your friend, and make sure you're on the train back by ten o'clock at the latest on Sunday, alright?"

I'd nodded, wondering how I was going to call – I'd lost the card to top my mobile up with.

There was a knock on my door, and it opened, just a crack. Helen. I smiled. "Come in."

She stepped into the room, pushing the door up, but leaving it open, just a little.

"I hear you're having an adventure today – are you all packed?'"" I nodded, holding up my rucksack. "Good. And have you put money on your phone?"

"I've lost the card for that." I wanted to cry – I felt as thought I'd done wrong, and people would be angry with me.

Helen smiled, and sat down beside me on the bed. "That's okay – do you remember I explained you could use your debit card?"

I'd forgotten – the tablets I took sometimes made it hard for me to remember things. "I'd forgotten, " I said, shaking my head. "But, now you've said, I do remember."

Helen smiled. "Do you want to do that while I'm here, then? In case you get muddled? You've got money in your account, haven't you? Your benefits came in alright yesterday?"

I nodded. "And I know I have to take money out for my rent on Monday."

"That's alright – when you go out to do your bits of grocery shopping, you can take the money out then, can't you?"

I nodded. "I should set up the thing Bridget talked about, where it goes out automatically. I'm sure I used to have those, when things were normal."

"If you want to set up a direct debit, I can come to the bank with you and help you do that – it would be useful, because it would save you having to remember."

"I never used to be this bad at things."

"I know, Morgana. It's okay – your brain is recovering from being under a lot of pressure. It's going to take time to get the wrinkles out, and, in the meantime, things are going to get lost in the creases. They'll pop back up again at some point, though, probably when you least expect it. Right – let's get this phone topped up, shall we? We can't have my star pupil getting into trouble because she doesn't have the money to call people, can we?"

### Maevynne Hanson

"I honestly can't believe you've never been in a health food shop
in – how long have you lived here?"
Tony grinned. "Too long."
"I'll bet you've been in McDonald's, though?"
"Plenty of times – though I prefer Chinese, to be honest."
I rolled my eyes. "Do you ever cook for yourself?"
"Yes – I'm not completely incompetent."
From the other side of the kitchen, I was aware of Feroc glaring at
me. "Just because he's not a vegan, taking a hundred and one
supplements a day, Maev, it doesn't mean he's scum."
"I never said -"
"You didn't have to say it." My brother's voice was quiet, lethally
so. "The whole way you've been with him, since you got here,
shows it. You don't like him because he's fat, and you think fat
people are thick."
I went to rush out a denial – and then blushed as I realised that
Feroc's accusation was more accurate than I was comfortable
admitting. My blush deepened when Tony Raglan turned away –
not quickly enough to cover the humiliation that had flashed in his
eyes.
"I'm sorry -"
"Don't be. It's only what everyone else thinks."
"No, it's not!" Feroc sounded quietly furious. I could see that he
was itching to be up and out of his wheelchair, so that he could
cross the room to stand beside his... Boyfriend? Partner? Lover?
What do gay couples call each other, anyway?
Tony sighed. "It is, Feroc. Everyone pretends it's not, but that just
confirms that it is – they think I'm too thick to notice."
"No." It was a moan, a refusal to believe. Tony smiled, sadly, and
I felt a stab of pure agony as I saw the hurt and bewilderment in
his eyes.
"Yes, Fer." His voice was a whisper, a caress. "But I have to deal
with it, to pretend not to notice, not to care. After all -" his voice
was bitter now "- this is my choice, isn't it?"

I'd always believed that, that people who were overweight chose to be, that it was down to laziness, but here, in my brother's kitchen, with his partner standing there, battered, bruised, and broken, yet still determinedly defiant, I heard the faint sound of convictions crumbling.

 I needed to make amends, and had a sense that I knew how to at least make a start.

"Tonight...when you go to meet your friend – do you want me to drive you there, and bring Feroc? I can stay out of the way, if you want me too, but it occurred to me you might like him there?"

 His smile brightened. "I'd like that very much, Thank you."

I smiled back. "I'll tell you what – if you let me make you a quinoa and fruit salad today, I'll let you make me your most indulgent, sinful comfort food tomorrow. And I'll eat as much of it as you manage to eat of the healthy option tonight."

His smile broadened. "Sounds fair. Just one thing, though."

"What?"

"I'm a Heathen – we don't believe in sin."

## RAGNAROK

For the time being, I'd put my research into my next proper victim on hold. I needed to go after the cop who'd found Andrew Jackson, first.

I'd found out where he lived, that was easy enough. They'd mentioned in the news that he'd been recently injured – as it turned out, in the accident involving the old woman who'd sped off after she'd seen me. I'd wandered round town until I spotted him.

He was with a younger woman, his girlfriend, maybe, coming out of the health food shop on the High Street. I'd followed them back, casual and calm, and walked past on the other side of the road as they'd gone into their house. Excelsior Street, number eighty. The one with the dragon decal on the upstairs window.

I'd been watching that house all day, sitting on the low brick wall that surrounded the block of flats a short way down the road. I wasn't the only person just sitting around, apparently doing nothing – this was Lothing, where dossers always had company.

It was early evening now. I'd give it until about nine, and then I'd call it a day. Injured people weren't usually inclined to go clubbing, after all.

## P.C. Tony Raglan
## LB 265

"Sorry – I'm just not that hungry for some reason."
Feroc reached out, stroking the back of my hand with his fingers.
"Are you feeling okay? Do you want to text this Morgana, ask her
to come here instead? You look rough – you probably shouldn't be
going out."
I laughed. "I'm not the one in the wheelchair. I'm fine, Fer – I just
feel a bit off colour, that's all."
He glared at his sister. "It's not her, is it? With what she was
saying earlier?"
"Like I haven't heard worse. Look, Fer, it's not exactly going to
kill me if I don't eat as much as usual for a day or so. Or, as
Maevynne there would undoubtedly say, even a month or so."
"If you're not eating normally by the middle of next week, I'm
calling the doctor in."
I rolled my eyes. "If I'm wrong about Morgana, I could be dead by
the middle of next week."
"WHAT?!"
I'd forgotten Maevynne wasn't in on things. Somehow, I thought it
was probably best to ensure that she didn't know the whole truth.
Upsetting the driver is never a good idea.
"Joke," I grinned. "Morgana's an old friend I haven't seen for a
while. Some people who've been in touch with her recently were
claiming she's become quite bitter and angry at the world – I told
them it couldn't happen, not to Morgana."
"Ah. Right." Maevynne looked uncomfortable. "Because, much as
I was prepared, on actually seeing you, to not like you -"
"You've realised it's hardly practical to give up your job to take
care of Feroc."
"I don't need taking care of. I'll be out of this chair in two weeks,
max."
"Yeah – and then you'll need to be looked after while your body
starts to actually heal. Trust me on this – I think I know what I'm
talking about."

Maevynne nodded. "He's right. The body doesn't actually heal while it's still in physical trauma – and, to a normally healthy person, being in a wheelchair is a physical trauma. The healing starts when the body is able to begin its normative processes again." She looked at me. "You know, the first we – my family and I – knew of you was when the news reported on your shooting, and showed that photo of you on the beach, where Feroc has his arm around you."

I smiled. "I think that was the first Feroc knew about me being more than a colleague and a mate. When he thought I might die." I looked at her, both wanting and not wanting to know the answer to the question I was about to ask at the same time. There's a rule in police interviews, albeit unwritten, that you never ask a question you don't already know the answer to. And I didn't know the answer to this one.

"Did you... I mean, Feroc had..."

She laughed. "Yes, we knew he was gay. He told us on his eighteenth birthday. Mum told him to wait until he was twenty-one. He sent her a text, at midnight on his twenty-first birthday, just saying "It's still dudes." She looked at me, and I knew what she was about to ask. For some reason, everyone who asked that particular question always had the same look, just before they finally decided it might be okay to ask it.

"When did you..? If that's not a personal question?"

"It is, but it's not one I mind. When I was a kid – eighteen, nineteen, twenty-one – I thought I must be crazy. I didn't think I could possibly be attracted to men. I mean, I wasn't naïve, I knew there were gay people, but I assumed they were all really effeminate men, who talked in high voices and wore make up. I wasn't like that, so I couldn't be gay. I was almost thirty before I realised you didn't have to be effeminate, or even camp, to be gay, and thirty-five before I had my first relationship." I caught Feroc's look, a struggle between wanting to respect my privacy, and wanting to know. I smiled, and decided to do the decent thing, and put him out of his misery.

"His name was Dan. We were together for a couple of years. It ended amicably enough – we just..." I shrugged - "we just ran out of things to talk about. Dreams to dream. I was single for three years after that, and then I met Max. We almost made it to the half-decade. A couple of flings, less than six months each, and then nothing. And then there was you." I looked over at Maevynne. "The stereotype isn't always true. Most of us, especially the older guys, don't have sex with anything in trousers, on a near-constant basis. We're much like anyone else – we want to have the shared record collection, the duplicate copies of books, the happy ever after." I glanced at my watch. "We should start to think about making a move. I just hope she turns up."

## RAGNAROK

I was just starting to think about calling it a night when they came out, the copper, the woman, and a young guy in a wheelchair. He looked a little older than the woman, but only a little – two, three years, maybe.

Probably her brother, I thought, having to live with them because he couldn't get a job, so couldn't manage on his own. I hoped his sister would be able to support him, once the copper was out of the way.

I felt  briefly guilty about what I was going to do – would I have chosen differently, if I'd known about the guy in the wheelchair? Perhaps. But, then again, perhaps not. The copper was a risk, and I had to be ruthless when it came to risk management – one of the struggles of working for yourself.

I watched as they got into a car – nothing special, a generic Vauxhall – a Vectra, maybe. It took a while, what with helping the guy in the wheelchair out of his chair, and into the front of the car. It looked a tight fit for the big copper in the back seat.

As the woman swung the drivers' door closed, I loped over to my own car, and we pulled out together, a physical rendering of harmony in motion.

## P.C. Tony Raglan
## LB 265

Something about the car that pulled out behind us nagged at me –
I could see it in the rearview mirror, and somehow, it looked
familiar, and in a way that made me feel strangely uneasy.

In the front passenger seat, Feroc caught my reflection in the
rearview, and turned a worried gaze on me.

"What's up?"

"The car behind us." He checked the rearview mirror, and the
wing mirror. "The Romeo?"

A blinding flash – a blood red sunset, shaped like a falling heart.
Romeo. Rome-ee-o. Lovers. Romance.

"What? "

"The Alpha Romeo -is that the car you meant when you said 'the
car behind us'?"

Alpha. A wolf pack. An Alpha wolf. A dark wolf, framed against a
sunset, making it look like a heart. No, not just a dark wolf – a
black wolf. Black like the car that was following us, tinted
windows and all.

I felt a chill run down my spine. "I've seen that car before." As
though conjured by the words, the memory came, something I'd
seen without seeing, the black Alpha Romeo passing me, heading
back to Lothing, as I'd been walking to Denes Wood the night
before.

"Where?" There was anxiety in Feroc's voice, now – he must have
picked up on my own. Maevynne glanced between us, sensing
that something was wrong, but with no possible way of knowing
just *how* wrong.

I swallowed, and checked on the Romeo's progress. Still with us.
We'd be at the beach in two minutes.

"Yesterday. It was heading back to Lothing as I was walking to
Denes Wood."

Feroc processed this. "And now it's following us." His voice was
calm – too calm. I spoke that calmly, when I was in the middle of
utter chaos.

I nodded. "And now it's following us."

We pulled onto the short run of parking that was technically reserved for the businesses along the pier side – at this time of night, though, none of them were open, and nobody was likely to be around to enforce anything as trivial as parking regulations. Maevynne cut the engine, and turned to me.

"What do you mean? What is going on?"

The Alpha Romeo pulled up just behind us. I took a deep breath. "I don't know – but I think you and Feroc should stay in the car."

"No way!"

I laid my good hand on Feroc's shoulder. "Feroc – please. Just do as I say. Pretend we're at work."

His eyes scanned my face. "You're serious, aren't you? You really believe that the driver of that car is... What *do* you think they are?"

The answer came at once, coolly and calmly, and with absolute conviction. "A murderer."

"Surely we should call the poli-" Maevynne trailed off, realising that I, and her brother, *were* the police.

"That's not a bad idea, actually. Feroc, call Wyckham, and ask him, ever so nicely, but making sure he knows it's somewhat important, it he could possibly spare a TSG unit down here? Tell him I know it won't look good in the papers, but there's no tourists, this time of night. Well, a few in the pub, maybe, but they should stay there."

I was shaking, and I could feel the sweat sliding down my body, even though I felt cold. Shock. PTSD. The pub I'd mentioned wasn't the Heart of Darkness – but the Heart of Darkness was only yards away. We'd passed it, coming down.

Guns, all over again. Was this going to be the signature for the rest of my life? I could hear the radio transmission in my head, the one call that always came out in a panicked rush, no matter how calm you tried to be: *Shots fired: Officer down.* Had that call been made that night two years ago? Had Feroc or Wyckham, or Aimee Gardiner, had their radios on them?

As everything faded around me, I got out of the car. Slowly.

## Morgana

I saw Tony, getting out of a car that I didn't think was his. I was
about to run over to him, about to call his name – and then I saw
the way he was looking at the other car, the black car that had
parked behind him.

 He was afraid.

I'd never seen Tony Raglan frightened before, and it looked wrong
– more wrong, even, than the sling on his right arm, and the way
he walked, slowly, one foot dragging behind him, like an old man
walking towards death.

 I watched him for a moment longer, then turned and watched the
black car.

 The driver's door opened. I tensed, looking around me to see if
anyone else had noticed. In the marina, the other side of the
Wharf, the *Mincarlo* rocked and lapped in her berth.

 The Wharf was a nice pub, designed to look a little bit like a boat,
on the inside. I was sitting outside. People were talking, laughing.

 A woman got out of the black car, and I felt the hairs on the back
of my neck stand up. When you live on the streets, you get good
at reading energy, and there was something very badly wrong
about hers.

 Quietly, I slid my empty lager bottle under the table, and broke it
with a single, sharp crack. A couple of people looked up, but by
that point, I was already on my feet, moving towards Tony and the
woman as though I were in a dream.

 I didn't really know what I was going to do – I just knew I had to
get there quickly.

## P.C. Feroc Hanson
## LB 599

"Feroc – what are you doing?"
I sat back, wincing in pain, having retrieved what I wanted from
the glove compartment. Maevynne was a journalist – she always
had a voice recorder in the car. I remembered that from the times
I'd visited her in Cambridge.
"Bring the window down."
"Feroc -"
"If this is what I think it is – if that woman is who I think she is – I
need to get this on tape. For Tony's sake."
"Is she this Morgana woman?"
I shook my head. "No. I think she's the person we all thought was
Morgana. I think she's worse than Morgana, because I think she's
*truly* insane."
Maevynne picked up on the stress. "This woman, Morgana, is
insane?"
"Possibly, but only temporarily so. Please, Maevynne, bring the
window down."
Finally, she did so, and, as unobtrusively as possible, I stretched
my arm out of the window, clicking the "record" button on the
machine I held lightly in the palm of my sweating hand as I did
so.
 And then I saw her, the woman who had to be Morgana Cassidy,
striding towards the black car, a broken bottle in her hand.

## RAGNAROK

"You rather upset my plans, Mr. Policeman."

He looked at me, like a wolf deciding whether a particular deer was worth pouncing on. "Really? I take it Andrew Jackson wasn't supposed to be found that quickly, huh?"

"I didn't care how quickly he was found – I survived Claire Jakely being found quickly – but, like her, he was supposed to be found by a clueless member of the public. Not someone who knew exactly who to call."

"And not someone who knew the significance of *Fehu*. You're not a caster, are you? It doesn't mean anything to you."

I smiled. "But it clearly does to you. How very ... unusual. A police officer who believes in magic."

"Not magic. Human potential, and the occasional assistance of beings that are ... other than human."

I laughed out loud, throwing my head back to give full voice to the sound. "Gods? You think your gods can he -aggghhhgakk...gakk..."

 I was aware of blinding pain, of everything fading and swirling, suddenly becoming far too bright, then far too dark...and then I was aware of nothing any longer.

## Morgana

She'd shown me her throat, jugular pulsing like a neon sign over a strip club – god, I'd seen so many of those places, too many. Too much, too often. Too loud, too bright. She'd shown me the sign, beating the path I needed to take, and I'd taken it with a frantic scream, charging in, slashing down with the jagged edge of the green, broken bottle.

I'd tripped on something – a loose stone, an untied shoelace, I didn't know what – and the edge of the bottle, pushed by the force of my fall, went deep into her throat, pushing through skin and muscle and fibre before the end of the bottle I was holding shattered in my hand.

I saw the blood, but didn't feel the pain.

I didn't feel the pain, but I did see the black shapes, big, darker than the night, and I heard their shouts, drowning out my own shouting.

They had guns. I wanted to get down on the ground, like they were telling me to, but I couldn't let go of the bottle. Even thought it hurt, I couldn't let go of it.

But I wanted to do what they were shouting at me to do. I really, really did.

## P.C. Tony Raglan
## LB 265

The woman was close enough to me for her blood, hot and sticky and richly red, to spray up into my face, falling like some kind of Ragnarokian rain, like the blood of my gods, all slain at once and beyond hope of resurrection.

I heard Morgana screaming, a long, wild wail of endless frustration, pain, and rage.

I heard myself screaming her name, tasting blood as it dripped onto my tongue.

And I heard the deeper, angrier, more threatening shouts, the shouts Morgana and I both needed to obey, but for some reason couldn't.

*"Armed police! Get down on the ground! On the ground, now! Now! Get down!"*

I couldn't move. Morgana didn't move, not until the woman finally dropped, when Morgana seemed to drop with her, not lying down of her own volition, but falling like a stone. I could hear her sobbing, almost drowning out the bellowed command I still couldn't bring myself to follow.

Suddenly, there were arms wrapping themselves around my waist. I hadn't seen or heard anyone approach, being blinded by the armed officers, who were still shouting, advancing forwards, weapons raised.

I kicked backwards, blind, and a sure, heavily-booted foot caught my ankle. We went down together, my unseen assailant and I, and, as we hit the paving slabs, and I saw the tiny LEDs that lit up the fountains, as I saw the jets preparing their shimmering moonwards leap, he growled something, close to me ear, rough, but not violent.

"You can be a bloody fool, sometimes, Raglan."

I sighed with relief. "Sir."

Arms still clasping my waist, Bill Wyckham nodded, his stubble rough against the side of my neck.

"Too damn right, Raglan."

## Inspector Bill Wyckham
## LB 81

So, as usual, TSG – the Thick and Stupid Group, as they were commonly known – had arrived on scene too late. Seeing this, they'd still wanted to shoot someone, to prove to the politicians that, even though terrorists were unlikely to be able to find Lothing, much less consider it worth attacking, their salaries were still justified.

As usual, I'd arrived just in time, and been surprised at how easy it was to take down a man of Tony Raglan's size. And been disappointed that I'd lost a long-running bet with Mark Roscoe – I'd maintained, for the past six or seven months, risking fifty quid I could have put to much better use on the deal, that Tony Raglan's bulk was mostly muscle.

Once the fall out from tonight settled, finally and forever, I was going to give Raglan hell for losing me that money.

Ambulances were called, and Morgana and the woman who, according to the vehicle check on her car, was a Ms. Eloise Mountfield, were taken to hospital, where the former was sectioned, probably indefinitely, as I was grimly informed by the tired-looking psychiatrist who'd been called away from a black tie dinner to deal with her, while the latter was pronounced DOA: Dead On Arrival. A severed carotid artery will do that, so the ghoulishly cheerful medical student who'd been on duty at the time we decided to upset the drunks of Lothing by making them wait a bit longer with the arms they'd broken falling off tables, and the noses they'd smashed knocking seven bells out of each other, informed me.

Tony was checked over by a First Responder at the scene, and, in shock, and his previously only badly cut and bruised arm now broken, driven to St. Raphael's in the front seat of my car. Aimee Gardiner took statements from Feroc and Maevynne Hanson, and a half-dozen good folk who'd been drinking quietly at the Wharf at the time of the incident.

We'd been wrong. We'd been almost fatally wrong, and Tony Raglan had been right.

He'd also quite clearly lied to me about not being in contact with Morgana – she'd disappeared off the map: there was no way she could have been in Lothing all these years, and the only reason she would have even thought about coming back was if someone had called her here. And the only person she cared enough to come back for was Tony Raglan.

I sat at my desk, the morning after the night before, my head in my hands, a mug of coffee cooling, forgotten, beside me.

A firm rap on the door had me raising my head. "Come." It sounded shattered, even to my ears.

The door opened slowly.

"Just wanted to see if you were alright. Hell of a night, by all accounts."

I gave Mark Roscoe a weary smile. "Yes. Lots of chickens coming home to roost, that's for sure. Oh," I rummaged for my wallet. "I owe you fifty quid."

"What?"

"Tony Raglan -"

"Again, I have no idea what you're talking about, Bill. And, speaking of Raglan, I owe you and him an apology – I was wrong, about Morgana Cassidy."

"You were."

"Your boy almost died because of it. And I truly am sorry about that, Bill."

I got to my feet, feeling as though I were moving through quicksand. "I know you are, Mark. It's okay. We all screw up sometimes."

"Yeah. I guess we do."

We stood in silence for a while, two men with so much to say, we'd run out of words.

Finally, Mark Roscoe broke the silence. "Well, like I say – I just dropped by to make sure you were okay, after last night."

"I'm fine. It's Tony Raglan you should go and see."

"I will."

## P.C. Tony Raglan
## LB 265

"I still don't know why I froze out there. I mean, every idiot knows, you've got armed officers pointing guns at you, screaming at you to get down on the ground, you get down on the ground."

"Ground! On the ground!"

Maevynne glanced at Idaho. "Does he ever shut up?"

I laughed. "Not so's you'd notice."

Feroc shook his head. "You were in shock. The bloody animals should have seen that. They should've stopped shouting. I don't even want to think about what would have happened, if Wyckham hadn't taken you down like he did."

"I know." I shook my head. "I'm just glad I wasn't able to lash out properly – I had no idea who it was. I hadn't seen anyone, hadn't heard anyone – I just suddenly felt someone grab me. I panicked, I could've really done him some damage. And got myself killed by TSG into the bargain."

Feroc laughed. "Oh yeah – he's not happy with you, by the way."

"Why? What've I done now?"

"Apparently, he had a bet with Roscoe, that you were stocky, rather than fat. That it was mostly muscle. He could've lost fifty quid, he reckons."

"Could have?"

"Roscoe doesn't remember the bet."

I was silent for a moment, my mind screaming thoughts I didn't really want to deal with at me.

"Out of curiosity..." Feroc sounded hesitant. I looked up, and saw him lick his lips. "How much *do* you weigh? It's okay if you don't want to answer – I'll understand."

I got to my feet, realising just how difficult taking most of my weight through one arm actually was, and turned to face Feroc.

"The last time I actually weighed myself, I was fifteen stone. If I'm more than that, now...." I paused for effect. "Then I'll give everyone in the nick who's interested twenty quid if I'm not back at that weight in a year."

Feroc grinned. "You're on – you do know the rest of them will want to make a formal event out your next weigh in, make sure you can't cheat them?"

"Make sure they've got an excuse for a piss up, more like. Alright, I'm not going to deny them their sport. I'll get it organised once we're both back – give me time to comfort-eat my way to acceptance of the reality."

"You're just making things harder for yourself," Maevynne chided. Feroc turned to his sister, smiling back at me over his shoulder. "Don't you know by now that's the way he likes it? He needs challenges."

I grinned. "Maybe not quite as many as I've had recently, though." Feroc gestured to Maevynne, who took hold of his chair, and wheeled him effortlessly across the room. I noticed, close too, how long his rakish blond hair was.

He held out a hand. I took it in my unbroken left hand, and, for a long several moments, we lost ourselves in each other's eyes.

"I love you, Tony – as you are, and as you will be."

My face felt suddenly wet, and, for a moment, I panicked, wondering if one of the several cuts on my head was bleeding again. It was only when I tasted salt that I realised Feroc's words had literally brought tears to my eyes.

"I love you, too, you bloody hippy." I tugged a lock of his hair. "Get that sister of yours to take you for a haircut, otherwise you'll be banned from setting foot in Lothing nick."

"Banned! Banned! Banana!" Idaho, not really understanding that words were run together in order to make sense, screeched and flapped in his cage, delighted at this opportunity to improve his vocabulary.

Feroc reached up, and ruffled my own hair, which was just getting long enough to irritate. "Speak for yourself, big man."

"Alright, we'll both be banned. And then what'll we do with ourselves? Can't exactly make a living sitting around watching *Countdown*, and I'm nowhere near old enough to retire."

"Really?" Feroc was all wide-eyed innocence. "I thought your next birthday was the one where the Queen sends you a telegram."

"Keep that up, kiddo, and your next birthday will be the one you celebrate on your own."

"Why, what're you going to do? Trade me in for an older model? I mean, you can't exactly go for a younger model, really, can you?"

"If you recall, you were the one who went for me."

Feroc grinned. "Yeah, well...I was hoping for a sugar daddy, only no one sent you the memo explaining how that's actually meant to play out."

"What, you mean a sugar daddy isn't someone who does his best to give you diabetes?"

On the sofa, accompanied by the parrot's demented screeching, Maevynne was chocking with laughter. Gasping for breath, she looked up, eyes shining with tears.

"Oh, god – you two are hilarious together."

I smiled. "So we're friends now, then?"

She smiled back. "Only if I get to join this list of people you might end up owing twenty pounds to."

"Done."

"And I want it on record, PC Raglan, that I will be very upset if I end up getting my money."

I laughed. "Your concern has been noted, madam. Now, if you'd kindly move along, perhaps into the kitchen, and make these poor broken lads a nice cup of something warm, wet, and ideally caffeinated, that would be much appreciated."

"And if I don't?"

"I'll nick you for resisting my partner's best interests." The smile Feroc gave his sister was all sweetness. I grinned. "Milk, three sugars."

"You'll have two, and be grateful – the sooner you get used to losing weight, the better."

"It's not definite that I'll have to yet." I picked up the TV remote, sat down, and clicked through to the afternoon Western on Channel 4. "I might still be fifteen stone. You never know."

Even the bloody parrot didn't stop laughing.

Printed in Great Britain
by Amazon